UNTOUCHABLE

Michael J. Martineck

Our Little Secret Press

Untouchable

Copyright © 2020 Michael J. Martineck

All rights reserved.

ISBN: 9798672847238

Our Little Secret Press

Cover design by Cole Johnson

Editing and formatting by Nina Martineck

For Sarah and Nina,
because smiles are the art I appreciate most

CHAPTER ONE

It looked like Marie Antoinette had thrown up in here. All the lush and layered drapery, white enamel and gold leaf, the room had rounded curlicue everything—every edge, corner and cut. Leah Capello knew the hotel charged more per night than she took home in a month. She'd looked it up. She wanted to look up the champagne on the table, next to the cheeses and real silver knife, but she needed to watch the two men standing across from her with suits so nicely tailored they seemed almost fake. There should have been a little rumple somewhere. The thought of having to put a bullet through one of those suits . . .

Two other men stood next to her. Special Agent Dean Jaworski served as her partner today. Allen Murkle served as their vouch – the person introducing them to other two. A small, hunched man, not quite sixty, but not hitting the gym often, ever, never in his life. She didn't want him in the room anymore. The two in the just-fit pinstripes were unsettled. They had done these exchanges enough times to know when something wasn't right.

That would be Dean and herself. They weren't right, depending on your point of view.

"Shall we begin?" Allen said, straightening his hunch and motioning to the easel next to him, draped in yet more velvet. As if this room needed any more swank.

"A moment," the younger and smaller of the two men facing Leah said, Russian accent more of a trickle than a Volga. 38 years old, six-foot-one, 165 pounds, Stepan Markov had inherited just over half of the Russian bauxite business when his dear father fell ill of 19 bullets. Leah had been unaware, until reading his file, that bauxite could create a net worth of $20.1 billion, American.

"Is there a problem?" Allen asked, smiling through his annoyance.

A knock came from the hotel room's front door.

"I'm thinking no." Markov smiled and glanced at the man next to him. The big guy, who had been introduced as Yuri, backed up and moved to the door with a fluid, controlled motion.

Leah took a half-second to glance at Dean. He made it clear, through the slightest of flinches, that he had not been expecting anyone else. He didn't have to say anything. In an operation like this one, the unexpected meant trouble.

Yuri put his big head to the tiny lens in the door, then leaned back, opened it and positioned himself to be behind whomever entered. He kept his arms at his sides. He was at the ready, Leah thought. A stance. This meeting had just tipped a little farther to the wrong.

Her head tilted a little to the right. Her eyes widened. Slightly. She caught them and her head, before she went all construction-worker on this guy and whistled as he passed. Hair like the surf at midnight, rolling over a rich olive complexion. Just a shade of beard—a hint to make you think he didn't try too hard. As if he had to try at all. Crap, Leah thought. Look at the little curls where his lips meet. A smirk? A dare? He watched her watch him.

She looked away.

"Who is this?" Allen asked with an edge. The Russians wouldn't like that edge.

"Joshua Fawls," the man said, entering the dead center of the room. The worst place to be, Leah thought. Either he didn't know that, or—she had the slithery, unfounded hunch—he didn't care.

A blue window-pane suit, as nicely constructed as the Russians', accentuated his narrow build. Leah ran her internal list: early thirties, six-foot, 175 pounds, no distinguishing scars or tattoos. He moved with confidence bordering on affected. He didn't seem too concerned with the population of the room. Except her. He glanced at her again. By reflex, she ran down her own list. Thirty-one, five-seven, mumble, mumble pounds. This stupid outfit. Black slacks, white blouse, gray jacket. Gray! Hair in a ponytail, like a literal pony's tail, black and barely done. Because ponies don't care.

Like you *don't care*, Leah shouted at herself, careful not to say it out loud. *You're working here.*

Joshua Fawls stopped before the easel. He clasped his hands behind his back. He wore white cotton gloves. He didn't put them on, as Leah often saw appraisers do, when they were going to examine an antiquity, which this was not. He'd already had them on.

Allen rolled the drape back over a painting. *Sea*, by Renoir. A vibrant seascape. His only one. No one outside of whoever stole it had seen it since 1990.

Allen's mouth moved like a snake. He presented the painting with open hands. A magician preparing you for a trick. Yuri stepped back to the circle. He noted everyone, as a very good bodyguard should. Joshua Fawls brought up his left hand, leaving its glove behind in his right. He leaned in and touched the Renoir. Allen gasped so Leah didn't have to. Dean flinched in the easel's direction, and checked himself before making an actual lunge. Leah wanted to see this Joshua guy's face, what he was doing, how close he'd gotten. He didn't move his hand around, trying to feel the brushstrokes or the grain of the canvas. He left it in one place, palm flat. He bowed his head, like she'd seen people do at the Vietnam Memorial, when they'd found a loved one's name.

He raised his head, took two steps back and said, "What an exquisite fake."

"I beg your pardon," Allen snapped.

"We're done here," Markov stated.

"Sorry, Stepan," Joshua said to the Russian.

"No, no," he protested. "It is why I have you around."

"This is absurd!" Allen stepped into the middle, directly in front of Joshua. "I don't even know you and I know everyone. I'm not going to stand here and let some— what are you? Some art student from Soho?"

"I am the man Mr. Markov asked to examine your knickknack," Joshua said. "And he was wise to do so."

"You declare this a forgery after thirty seconds of examination?"

"It took me ten," Joshua said. "The rest was for show." He glanced at Markov. "I can't make it look too easy."

"I appreciate that," Markov said.

Allen turned to Markov. "I assure you—"

"You assure me of nothing."

Leah watched the big guy, Yuri. He continued to stand with his hands at his sides, tight and ready.

"And you, Mr. Jaworski." Markov looked at Dean. "I do not think we will be doing anymore future business."

Leah knew that was coming. This whole operation—ten months of nips, dabs and secret emails, whispers at parties, flights across the northern hemisphere—poof. Gone. Thanks to this—

"Interloper." Allen's voice strained. "I have spent nearly fifty years developing my skills. On what are you basing your finding?"

Joshua lowered his head a few degrees. Not in supplication, Leah decided. More like aim. "I get paid for that information. Right now, my client is Mr. Markov. If you would like a consultation, make an appointment. It would appear you could benefit from some insight."

"Thirty million dollars at stake," Allen spat. "I think I deserve an explanation."

"You are funny," Markov said. "I am thinking *I* need an explanation. You were trying to take me for thirty million dollars."

"I was not," Allen said. "The painting is genuine."

"Thirty million," Markov repeated. "But that is not what hurts me."

"I'm not hurting anyone."

"All right," Dean said, "Maybe we can take this down a notch."

"You fellas . . ." Joshua turned and gave Leah a wide, warming grin. "And the lady, can do whatever you like."

Joshua rotated at the hip to face the Russians. Leah thought he might bow, all theatre-like, but Allen grabbed his arm. Joshua tried to shake it loose and Allen swung and smashed the taller, younger, much much much more toned Joshua Fawls across the face. The man had not seen it coming. No one did. No one ever could have. They were not dealing heroin, here. This was freakin' art.

Joshua toppled to the table, hitting the edge. The champagne and glasses rattled. *Shit*, Leah yelped in her head.

Yuri's gun was out, leveled at Allen. Dean drew his sidearm and aimed straight-armed at the big Russian. Leah had her duty pistol out before she'd even thought about it, also aiming at the room's number one threat. Allen did the single stupidest thing she'd ever seen a person do. He grabbed the silver knife off the table and swished in behind the still stunned Joshua. He put it to the man's throat. An art dealer. For Christ's sake.

She moved to smack Allen's arm down, but he spun, arching Joshua around, putting Joshua between him and all the guns.

"Allen," she shouted. "What the crap?"

"Stay back." He started back towards the hotel room door.

"Drop the knife." She tried to find a spot on him she could hit without killing the hostage. "You're being ridiculous."

"Do you know who these men are?" He reached behind him with one arm, using the other to press the blade to Joshua's throat. It might not be that sharp. Then again . . .

"The deal went south." She moved closer. Yuri had his black automatic on Dean now. Markov stood motionless. Dean didn't make it into her peripheral vision. "This isn't worth it."

Allen opened the door to the hallway. "Mr. Markov does not let things lie."

"So what are you going to do?" Leah asked.

"First." Allen backed out of the room, dragging a very still and steady Joshua. "I'm going to get the hell out of here."

Leah followed them out into the hall. Allen inched along, knife to Joshua's throat, left arm holding Joshua's wrist. The angle didn't give the man any leverage. Leah kept her pistol up and aimed. Would she have to shoot this bastard over a bad painting? She couldn't let him split this art expert's jugular. This blew. So bad. The elevators were about twenty-five feet away. A turn to the left. Maybe he'd make a mistake. Maybe he'd—

"Wha—?" Allen fell backwards, arms flying wide. Joshua rolled to his left, out of the way. A silver coffee urn shot towards Leah, skipping on the carpet. She didn't shoot. Allen landed hard from the fall and Joshua stepped on the wrist that held the cheese knife.

"He's all yours," Joshua said, staring down at the art dealer.

She closed the gap, gun in both hands, pointed at Allen's midsection. "You alright?"

"Him or me?" Joshua said.

Leah ignored him. He seemed fine. "Crap, Allen," Leah said. "You're under arrest."

"You're a cop?" Joshua asked.

"FBI," Leah said.

"Honestly," Joshua said, "I overcharge and the Russian is *still* not paying me enough. Do you have a badge?"

Leah drew a leather wallet with credentials out of her jacket pocket and handed it to Joshua. She said to him, "You step back." Joshua moved off of Allen's wrist. To Allen she said, "You roll over."

Allen winced and rolled onto his stomach.

"A coffee urn left in the hall? Really?" Leah said. "Are you like the luckiest man alive?"

Joshua's eyes blinked too slowly. They looked heavy, dragging, dramatic. A show. A good show, she had to admit, but a still a show. "I make my own luck." Joshua kissed Leah's badge and handed it back to her.

Eww? European? The weirdness would explain the lack of a wedding band.

CHAPTER TWO

Leah Capello did not like getting out of her comfy pants, but she didn't get called to a lot of crime scenes, either. The Federal Bureau of Investigation's Art Crime Team tended to find out about thefts, forgeries, and recoveries for days, years, or sometimes decades after the inciting incidents. In her two years with the Bureau, she'd never received a phone call from the New York City Police Department. She'd been pretty certain they didn't know she existed, let alone had an office in Manhattan. The peculiarity of it all just about made up for having to get back into the rayon slacks, finding a blouse that didn't look like she'd pulled it through a straw, and strapping on the belt—the thick leather that held her weapon and cut into her hips all day long.

She took a cab to the West 23rd address, opened her wallet for a showing of her badge, hung it from a black lanyard so she didn't have to keep flashing it to all the uniforms, and entered The January.

A uniform cop worked the door. Farther in stood a short, medium-build detective in his thirties, who might actually be happy she'd taken the ride across town. He didn't look too comfortable in the stark white maze, surrounded by $50 million worth of mixed media. He was speaking with what Leah thought to be the manager: a woman shy of fifty, size two, wearing heels that brought her to six-foot even, and the kind of tight black and white dress that catches your eye in the store. You hold it up and say "yeah, but when am I ever going to wear it?" Too nighttime for work, too chic for going out with friends, too clingy for a first date and there's only first dates in front of you at the moment, sweetie. *Art gallery manager*, Leah thought. That's when you wear that kind of movement-limiter. Leah might have owned one just like it herself a few years ago.

The space had been constructed to lure a buyer in, with three pieces of large, striking, very hip work mounted on thin walls and lit to intrigue. Intrigue landed you at the wall-shelf with a phone that they called the front desk. Pausing there one would be wordlessly pre-qualified, by the manager or her ilk, and then, if you seemed like you might possibly have twenty grand to twenty million to toss around, you would be sent into the run. A rat to be stimulated, sampled, and either rewarded or discarded.

Leah introduced herself to the detective. Roberts reciprocated, highlighting his newness to the Major Case Squad. The detective usually assigned to art theft wasn't available. Leah nodded. He introduced the manager, Ophelia.

Ophelia looked at her with eyelids a tad too close together. Leah knew the expression. She looked familiar to Ophelia and Leah didn't like to look familiar.

"It's nice to be called in on the ground floor," Leah said to the detective.

"Wish I could take credit for it," Roberts returned.

Leah held her hand out to Ophelia. "I must have you to thank."

"A very sorry 'no,'" she said, "Although I do feel we may have met."

"Have you been burgled before?"

"Never," Ophelia said, narrowing her eyes two microns more.

Roberts said, "The request came from our witness."

"Oh." Leah had no decent response. A witness that requested her? The weirdness had to wait. "What was taken?" she asked.

"An Anselm Kiefer," Ophelia said.

"Just the one?"

"Yes."

"You're sure only one painting is missing."

"Quite," Ophelia forced a smile.

"Any strong and unfulfilled interest in the work recently?"

Ophelia retained the smile across the lower half of her face. The upper half went into ethical distress. Leah understood. She'd been in her heels once or twice before. The economy of the art world had three mediums of exchange: art, money, information. The art world tried to convince itself that the importance ranked in that order. The reverse was, of course, the truth.

The knowledge of who wanted what could have more value than the actual 'what' in many cases. Artists fixed supply, making demand the movable variable. Cost was determined by whispers, proxies, hunches and trust. Ophelia's position in the art world was a function of her ability to keep and release secrets. Her livelihood—her self-worth, Leah knew all too well—came from her discretion. She couldn't like Leah testing it.

"There is always interest in all of our works," Ophelia said. "We would not hang a piece if it lacked appeal."

"I'm talking about a specific kind of interest," Leah said. "Did it really pique someone?"

Ophelia met Leah's stare. She blinked twice as her practiced smile morphed into a true, knowing one. "I knew I'd seen you before . . ."

Leah clenched all of her muscles, lightly, so as not to show. A good gallery manager had an exceptional graphic memory. It was a must. One had to keep, recognize and track art, naturally. One also had to recognize and track people. Buyers, artists, high-rollers, bottom-feeders, pretenders, offenders and clients truly interested in advancing a collection. All of this had to be done from a standing position, on the fly, all the time. The good ones could, and Leah now postulated that Ophelia might be better than good.

"You're the Turner girl, aren't you?" Ophelia finished.

"I go by Special Agent Capello," Leah returned.

"Of course." The fake smile slammed down.

The Turner Girl. Hot damn, she hated that. First off, she hadn't been a girl in, like, twenty years. And one brief encounter with one painting by one Romanticist was not going to define her entire life.

Nor would it define this moment.

Leah huffed. Maybe she could crack this woman, maybe she couldn't. For now, it might be best to keep her investigation broad. Broader than this broad. Broad strokes, Leah. Broad strokes.

Leah turned to Detective Roberts. "What did the video show?"

"Nothing," he said.

"How's that?"

"There was only one camera on that hallway. It got bumped sideways, so the playback shows nothing but the wall from 19:21 on."

Leah didn't bother fighting her facial expressions. She let them save her the trouble of saying this story made no sense.

"Seriously," Roberts continued. "The playback doesn't show anybody coming up to the camera and screwing with it. It just jerks sidewards and stays that way until we reposition it."

"And the door camera?" Leah asked. "What does that show?"

"Ok, alright, here's the thing. No one leaves."

"So the thief and the painting might still be here?"

"Damned if I know, ma'am."

"You can see why we called the FBI," Ophelia added.

Roberts said, "It's not the FBI's jurisdiction, but we figured you might have seen something like it before."

Now Leah suspended her expressions. She didn't need these two knowing she'd rarely been to an actual crime scene, never within an hour of the crime, and never ever heard of anything close to a freakin' magic show like this.

"So the witness," she started, "the one who had my name. He or she is still here?"

"Two witnesses, actually." Robert nodded towards the back of the gallery.

Leah left the desk and walked around the next thin wall. A gorgeous acrylic faced her on the far wall, small halogen lights bringing out the searing reds and blues. She didn't bother to glance at the works on either side. She walked to the end and turned right.

The big Russian stood facing her, from the corner. Same perfectly fit suit, same unnatural arms-at-the-sides stance, face stern to the edge of angry. Yuri.

Leah said, "I believe we have met before. About two months ago, at the Aventador Hotel?"

"You did," came from a little farther down. Stepan Markov gazed into the right wall. He cupped his right elbow with his left hand and his chin with his right. From this angle, Leah couldn't see what he saw. He wore a royal blue suit—this season's color—over a canary yellow shirt.

"I'm honored that you remember me." Leah strolled in Markov's direction.

"I don't believe there is man who wouldn't," Markov said.

Don't blush. Don't blush. He wouldn't see it anyway, right? Not in this perfect gallery light, crafted and balanced to bring out the most nuanced colors and textures.

"You are the witness?" She positioned herself next to him. He stared a wall, blank save for a nail and picture hanger.

"Yuri, too," he said. "We were here when the Kiefer vanished."

"Did you see who took it?"

Markov leaned his head very close to Leah's. "I need you to do something for me."

She leaned as well and said, "That is not an answer to my question."

"I will answer any question if you say you will do this thing for me."

"Do you know how criminal investigations work in this country?"

"I am experienced," Markov replied. "They are much the same in every country in which . . . I have noticed. You want this painting and I want this thing."

"Usually," Leah said, "witnesses just tell us what they witnessed."

"This is not the usual."

Leah stepped between Markov and the blank wall. She wished —
for the first time ever, maybe—that she'd worn heels. She had to look up
into his face. Not the effect she wanted. "What's the thing you want?"

He lowered his head. His eyes seemed sleepy. No. Tired. Whatever cockiness she'd seen in him before, whatever front he tried to put on
just now, did not go all the way to his slightly watering, very weary eyes.

"I need you to find Joshua Fawls," Markov said.

"Right, what?"

"You met him that time you tried to sting me."

"I remember him," Leah said. "Isn't he your associate? Doesn't
he work for you?"

"He is not answering his phone."

"Maybe he doesn't want to talk to you," Leah said. "I wouldn't
know why, you being the height of charm and all. Although there was that
time you got together and he almost got his neck split open."

"We have stayed on good terms," Markov said.

"If you think he's in trouble or missing—"

"I need him immediately." Markov's voice dropped like a rock.

"You seem like a man of means," Leah said. "What do you need
me for?"

"I need Mr. Fawls. I have since eleven this morning and have not
been able to locate him. Time is important to me or I would not have gone
to such trouble to bring you here."

Leah's nervous system lit up. She felt the surge of new chemicals,
the kind that help you run or bite or ignore a wound.

"Trouble?" she spat. "Bring?"

"I did not have time to find you," Markov said. "So I troubled to
have you come here?"

"Where's the painting, Mr. Markov?"

"Will you help me?"

"Where is the painting?"

"This must reinforce for you how important this thing is to me."

"You and Yuri are going to jail," Leah said. "And I don't think that puts you any closer to Fawls. Maybe. I don't know. Probably not. The painting."

Markov pointed his head in Yuri's direction, but kept his attention on Leah. "We should help the Special Agent, yes?"

Yuri walked behind Markov. He stopped next to the large painting hanging on that wall. A barn, done in shadows of brown and gray and black. Compelling, but spooky. Leah thought it might be another Anselm Kiefer. Yuri lifted the edge of the painting from the wall. A canvas slid out from behind and down to the floor. It curled a bit at each end but Leah could make out a head, floating above a bleak landscape, done in watercolor.

The missing painting.

CHAPTER THREE

Leah sat in the back of the Tesla S. She'd never been in one before, though she'd seen them often enough. The other coast had a species of art world player that found electric cars hip. Not so much in New York, but this Russian certainly didn't give up any luxuries. She slumped back in to the caramel leather seats and watched the city swish past.

"It's not very menacing," Leah said. "The car, I mean."

"Menacing," Markov repeated. "Like a man's car? You think this is not a man's car?"

"Menacing, like scary," Leah returned. "This is not a forceful car, like an Escalade or one or those big Mercedes."

"It's aluminum," Markov said. "I like to support my customers."

"No two liter bottles at the Markov's, huh."

Markov glanced at her, puzzled. She caught Yuri glancing at her, too. Through the rearview mirror.

"That detective did not believe your story." Leah decided to change the subject.

"By tomorrow, he will not care. The case is closed."

"How did you move the camera?"

"A small drone."

"Huh," Leah said. "Why?"

"So video would not see us."

"No, why bother half-stealing the painting in the first place?"

"I do not understand the question."

"This is pretty elaborate," Leah said. "Couldn't you just pay someone off to get my number?"

"Such things could happen," Markov continued. "They could happen with time."

"Which you don't have. So you've said."

"Thank you for your understanding."

Leah didn't understand. She did not understand one smidge of what had happened so far tonight. And it wasn't even nine. She didn't understand what this billionaire wanted, why he used a crazy-ass scheme to get in touch with her, or what could possibly be so important. Or so timely.

When in doubt, ask. "What's the deal, Mr. Markov?"

"Did I mention a deal?"

"Something's got you into some risky behavior. Now I'd be super flattered if you were trying to create your own twisted version of a meet cute. I'm thinking that's not the case. You are a businessman. Business deals don't call for an art expert like Fawls. Art deals call for an expert. So, again, I ask—what's the deal?"

Markov went back to looking out the window. Yuri had chosen 7th, which was smart this time on a Wednesday night. It took them through the Village, but it was still better than the West or 8th. This Yuri knew his stuff.

"If you could locate Mr. Fawls," Markov said. "I would forever be in your debt. I am a very good person to have in your debt. Most specially in your kind of work."

He had that right. Leah had clamped on to that factoid immediately. She also knew something else hung around them, caught in the gravity of her curiosity. She could not tell this man good-bye, go home, fire up the DVR and be done with it all. That was the only thing she knew for sure right now: that she wasn't done.

She asked Markov for his phone number and put it in her own.

They pulled up in front of Federal Plaza, it being one of the few places on the Island of Manhattan that one could pull up at any given time. Chess pawns the size of first-graders ringed the complex, and Federal police kept anyone stopping by from staying more than thirty seconds. The Murrah Federal Building explosion happened twenty-five years ago, and the government still hadn't gotten over it. Not that Leah minded. Safety first.

"I'll be in touch." Leah left the car, scooted across the sidewalk and entered the glass doors. The building appeared closed. That never really happened. Crime never slept, she'd been told, though she learned later that wasn't entirely true. Crime slept, the Bureau just never knew when.

Credentials, codes, an interminable wait for the elevator, more codes, and she rose to her office. What the Bureau called an office. She called it a cubby: a box, open on one side for shoes and pencils, that happened to be big enough for an adult human. Barely. Not that she minded this, either. She could almost do her entire job from her phone.

Almost.

As part of the FBI's Art Crime Team, Leah spent all of her time on missing works of art, antiquities and items of cultural significance. A missing person did not have a place on that list. The differences were huge.

So what the freak are you doing, Leah Natalena Capello? She yelled at herself as she sat down at her desk and fired up her computer. This was pretty close to unethical and totally crossed over into stupid.

It also helped her develop her very own civilian asset. A major player. Yeah, perhaps she was getting played right now, but the ask had not been painful. Find Joshua Fawls. She didn't have to turn him over. If Markov wanted the man so he could bust his kneecaps, well, she was doing Fawls a big favor by finding him first. She could be preventing a crime.

Something like that.

None of it mattered if she couldn't find the man, so the odds of this not mattering were excellent.

There are lots of ways to track a person. Markov had already tried the personal ones. He'd been to his apartment, his haunts, his friend— Markov only knew of one—and his other associates. No one had seen in him in days. Leah explained that the man could be anywhere on the planet. Markov disagreed. If Fawls lived, he lived in New York. She had no reason to trust him on that. She didn't have to. She needed to act like Fawls was alive.

And might very well have fallen into trouble. Art authentication did not have a storied history of violence, but he'd found some the last time they'd met. She had every reason to believe Fawls could be in danger—or so she could tell her supervising officer when he asked why the hell she'd requested a cellphone check for someone unrelated to the crime she'd been sent to investigate. If Fawls was in danger, things changed. She didn't need a court order to see if his phone was active.

Leah called in the request and received an answer almost immediately. The phone had been used to make a call last night, in midtown. The triangulation of the cell towers only gave her a two-block range. Those two blocks were home to some of the most sumptuous hotels this side of Central Park.

She had a working theory and it had nothing to do with an art deal gone bad. She searched-up a photo of Joshua Fawls, sent it to her phone and returned to the elevator.

The pool of cars in the basement of the Federal building did not excite Leah. She had no outsized love of cars. She had no outsized love for any tool that helped her do her job. Guns, computers, surveillance equipment—sure, it could all be cool. None of it a Rodin sculpture or a Calder mobile cool. Still, this accountant-designed sedan was an affront to aesthetics. Three boxes stuck together, with wheels cut into the sides. And God, she hated driving in the city. Lights and sirens barely made a difference, so she didn't bother. Markov might have been in a hurry to find Fawls, but she wasn't sure Fawls wanted to be found just yet.

Which did not stop her from zipping up to W. 59th as fast as the chunky stew of cars, trucks and buses between her and her swanky hotels, would allow. She would have preferred to make the trip in the back of Markov's car. She also would have preferred to know what he wanted with Fawls. Until she knew that, she figured she'd best keep them apart.

Leah parked in front of The New Juncture. More than a century old, it not only had a worthy art collection in the lobby, bars and public rooms, but it stood as a work of art all in itself. The Beaux Arts design featured American iconography, tying together the old world and new, creating a welcoming entrance for incoming foreign dignitaries and a fitting departure for nouveau riche off on their grand tours. Leah loved the cream and mocha lobby, a two story hug. The art cognoscenti tended to the love the place, too. So she started her search at its front desk.

Staff fetched the evening manager for Leah. The crisp young man moved them to a small office and Leah showed him her photo of Fawls. He quickly denied ever having seen him. Leah explained that she stopped by to remove a potential problem from his hotel without making a sound. She respected his discretion, but urged him to think about the concerns of all of his guests, including the ones that might find a SWAT team, rescue squads and a fleet of local news vans disturbing.

"A bit of intrigue can be good for business," the manager said with a thin grin.

"I know, right?" Leah agreed. "I have a friend who goes to haunted hotels on purpose. She seeks them out. Crazy. Of course, who am I telling. You probably see all kinds of crazy."

"I do." The manager nodded. "This city attracts them."

"Like bees to a soda can." Leah stood.

The manager stood as well.

"You've been very nice," Leah drew a business card from her pants pocket and handed it over. "I'm sure you have been as helpful as you thought you could be. If you ever find yourself with a soda can you can't seem to get rid of, you call me. I'll remember you."

She smiled and eased out of the room, into the marble hall that led to the lobby. She didn't look back, though she wanted to. She wanted to see if the young man looked at her card and weighed its value. An FBI agent owing you a favor. You. A night manager. It had to be worth something, right? It had to be worth a freakin' three digit number?

She kept walking and not turning and listening. The footfalls were soft. The manager hopped in next to her and matched her pace.

"We have a couple," he whispered. "They have not left the room in two days. They have declined all services. This is not highly unusual in and of itself. But one does worry."

"Let me check on them," Leah said. "Make sure they are alright."

"Room 323," the manager said.

Leah headed for the elevators.

CHAPTER FOUR

Knock, knock.

No answer. Leah stood close to the door, so she could see if the light in the peep hole changed. Which it did. She knocked harder. The door opened two inches, sliding along the safety catch.

"Yes?" A woman nearing thirty, with a ton of messed up hair—chestnut and a brush of gold—showed Leah half her face. She had great cheekbones, a small mouth and hadn't freshened her makeup in twelve hours. She knew that look all to well.

"May in come in for a moment?" Leah asked.

The woman's small mouth opened. Exaggerated incredulity. "I don't think so."

"No one has been in your room since Monday. I just need to check a few things."

"We're fine."

"Then you shouldn't mind me coming in for quick second. It won't take long."

"I said we're fine. We're in the middle of something."

"So there are more than one of you occupying the room?" Leah asked.

"Does that matter? I'm not allowed a guest?"

"May I speak with your guest?"

The woman's eyes narrowed to nearly nothing. Her little mouth went Cheerio. "You know my guest?"

"I don't know. Should I?"

"Fine." The woman slammed the door. Leah could hear the catch knock back. The door flew open. The woman stood to the side. Short midnight blue robe. Decent figure. Probably Yogalates three times a week and a hyper-A personality. "Let's get this over with."

Leah blew past her, but maintained visual contact. She hadn't been invited in for tea. Not that the woman could be concealing a weapon. She did have two inches on her, though. And attitude. The suite had a small lounge, with a nook to make drinks or coffee. She walked passed that to peer into the sleeping area.

The bed had a man, spread eagle, under a sheet. She caught the glint of metal around the wrists. Handcuffs? He lifted his head.

"Mr. Fawls," Leah said. "Are you—"

Something hit her from behind. Something heavy and hard and she launched forward, stumbling. She wanted to stop her fall. Nothing to grab.

"Marisa!" Joshua shouted. "She's FBI!"

"Son of a bitch!" the woman shouted.

Got that right, Leah shouted back, in her head. She hit the floor and rolled. She looked up in time to see a silver tray sailing at her head. Frisbee style. This would hurt.

Leah fell flat on her back from the impact. She actually saw stars. Flashes. Like a cartoon. *God, I'm a freakin' moron.* Leah rolled again, jumped up and pulled her sidearm.

The woman was gone.

She wanted to pursue. No one assaults a federal officer and slinks away. Certainly not that chick. She swayed. *Jesus forgive me, that hurt.* She looked at Joshua, cuffed to the bed.

"Are you OK?" he asked.

"Are *you* OK?" she asked back.

"I've been better."

Leah started towards the other room, ready to chase.

"Please," Joshua said. "She won't get far."

He looked so helpless. The droop of his eyes—not bedroom eyes, not a come-hither gigolo glance. More puppy-left-out-in-the-rain.

"Screw it." Leah put her pistol back in its holster, nestled just behind her right hip. She'd take care of the hostage first. Right? That's the play? She approached the bed.

"This is awkward," Joshua said.

"Your girlfriend's an asshole," Leah returned.

"She's not my girlfriend."

"Ok. Your best friend's wife is an asshole."

"That's hurtful," Joshua said. "I'm the victim here."

"Yeah." Leah reached the nearest handcuff, connecting Joshua to the left bedpost. "I can see you're in a lot of pain."

"Don't!" Joshua yelled.

Leah froze.

"There are gloves. Somewhere. You need to use them."

"No gloves, no love, huh."

"I'm serious. Really serious. Don't touch me."

Leah backed off. "Fine. I'm not here for the touching, sir."

"You can call me Joshua. I insist."

"And you can call me Special Agent Capello."

"Fair enough," Joshua said. "The gloves should be near the couch."

Leah shook her head as she walked back to the lounge. She went all the way to the door and closed it. She saw a pile of men's clothing in the corner. Two white gloves lay beside it. She snatched them up and slipped them on.

"Any idea about a key?" she called out.

"Knowing Marisa," Joshua shouted, "it's in her stomach."

Leah disagreed. She'd eventually want that guy's hands free. She found the little key on the table with the TV, next to the room card. She walked back into the bedroom. Joshua had let his head fall back. He couldn't see her, so she didn't mind looking him over, just him and his silk sheet. He must run or swim or something. Probably the something. This man was a supine Michelangelo's David. Exquisite.

"Crap," she said directed at . . . everything.

"Did you find the key?"

"Yeah. Whatever." Leah unlocked Joshua's right wrist. The skin beneath was raw, almost to bleeding. He shook his wrist and 'awed' in a way that made her uncomfortable. She walked around the bed, snugging the gloves. Gloves. No touching. Why were the cute ones always such whack jobs? She unlocked the left wrist.

"Oh God, thank you." Joshua rubbed the red rings as he sat up, letting the sheet settle on his lap.

"Glad to hear you say that. I wasn't so sure you wanted to be disturbed."

Joshua gather the silk, got off the bed and wrapped it around. He started stretching, bending and flexing his knees. "Check the bathroom."

Which she should've done right away. What an amateur. This guy persisted in knocking her off her game. She was a good agent. She was a good agent. She drew her gun again and rounded the door to the bathroom.

No one. The counter had a makeup case and a nickel-plated automatic.

"See a gun?" Joshua asked, continuing to furl and unfurl his limbs.

"Yeah." Leah put her gun away and faced him. "It's the hot accessory this spring."

"That's the gun Marisa used to kidnap me, bring me here and force me to do whatever she wanted."

"Wow." Leah let her mouth drift open and hang there for a bit. "That is not even close to . . . wow."

"You'd be treating this whole scene different if you'd found a woman chained to that bed."

"I should apologize," she said in a soft voice. She couldn't back it up with much emotion. None of this felt right.

"Don't apologize." Joshua stopped stretching, put his hands on his hips and looked directly at her. The cut of his lower abdominal muscles were like two arrows leading her eyes to the brink of the silk drape. She knew enough about composition and design not to be drawn in. She wouldn't fall for God's little tricks. "You rescued me," he continued. "I'm not going to make you feel bad about that. That would make me the asshole here."

"But not as big as the one that hit me with a tray. Twice."

Joshua smirked. "I'm going to, uh, find my clothes." He walked into the lounge.

Leah sat on the lower edge of the bed positioned so she could project her voice out into the other room. She rubbed her forehead. Only then did she remember she wore white cotton gloves. "You don't seem surprised to see me."

"Ah, yes," Joshua said. "Astonished. It's uncanny that you arrived right when I needed you."

"Not convincing. Does Markov have a connection to that woman? Marisa?"

"Markov? Stepan? No. No connection I know of, anyway."

"He has been very concerned about you."

"I couldn't say why. Marisa wasn't exactly holding me for ransom."

"He thought you might be in trouble."

Joshua reappeared, black pants on, but not fully cinched. He carried a purple and black checked dress shirt, which he proceeded to pull on. "He's used to having his texts returned."

"You are very popular," Leah said.

"With some more than others." Joshua buttoned his shirt. "I really need a drink."

"You don't want to come to the office? Maybe file a complaint?"

"And keep you on duty? I don't think so." He tucked his shirt in and fastened his pants. "You've done quite enough for tonight. Now, if you wouldn't mind removing those gloves and laying them on the bed."

Leah took the gloves off and set them on the mattress. Joshua leaned over to collect them. With his face only a few inches away, Leah said, "I've got questions."

"A good single malt always loosens my tongue," Joshua replied.

CHAPTER FIVE

The lobby bar at the New Juncture had been designed by beavers for beavers. Humans would never commit to this much wood. Cut, carved, curled and curated. Oak flooring, mahogany wall panels and more oak beams crisscrossing the ceiling. The bar, the shelves, the stools and tables—hickory, birch, rose. Leah's eyes were thrilled to find a standing army of glass bottles, at attention, sparkling and rich. An escape from the knots and grain. Maybe that was by design. The whole room served as a frame for those little works of art.

She had second, third and fourth thoughts about leaving a non-secured crime scene for a bourbon on the rocks. They fit nicely with her doubts about her whole evening. An art heist that wasn't. A kidnapping that wasn't. She didn't like fakery. The whole reason she joined the Bureau was her distain for fakes.

The distain started with the first crime scene she'd ever been to. As the victim, officially. More or less. She never took to victimhood. It didn't fit right. She felt fairly complicit in the crime. She'd been persuaded to put a substantial deposit down on a painting and the painting turned out to be a fake. A forgery, to be specific. Fakes could be accidental.

Someone can misidentify a work. It's easy enough to do, especially the wider the time gap between the work's completion and its attribution. A forgery is different. It's done with criminal intent. Someone puts a great deal of effort into creating a work of art they can attribute to someone else who will fetch a higher price. A Turner, for instance. A spanking-new gallery sales associate might be tricked into buying a painting that absolutely looked like a work by Joseph Mallord William Turner. The feathery spread of light and color, the dark whorls of London, the umber sunrise, reflecting in the unsteady waters of the Thames. Theme, setting, technique, media—it all fit so well.

Too well.

Dean Jaworski had been the special agent assigned to her case. He said this kind of thing happened all the time. In fact, he believed it didn't happen enough. If all the galleries— private and public—put all their works through the tests her gallery had just performed on the painting she just bought, the art world would vanish. A sand mandala: beautiful, precise and scattered in the wind. As long the art world remained a work in progress—its devotees adding ever increasing layers of detail—no one stepped back and took a good look at the big creation made by all the smaller ones. If they did, the invisible hand of the market would wipe it clean.

Dean thought a full third of the art around us was fake.

Leah didn't know about that. She spent too much of her life admiring the individual works. She didn't care to consider the work *Art World* as a whole. Her forgery had been one speck in the eye. Still, it left a scar.

Sometimes the scar throbbed. Like right now. In this bar. With the lovely Mr. Fawls. Doubt, doubt and double doubt. That last batch being of the "self" kind.

When in doubt, as she had been instructed at the Academy, stick to the training. Ask questions. Get answers. Ask more questions. Get more answers.

"Why did Markov want me to find you," Leah started, "if he didn't know you were being detained?"

"I don't know," Joshua replied.

"Is he angry with you? Another deal done bad?"

"We're still besties. Besties forever."

"Is he in some kind of trouble? The kind you might be able to help with?"

"I'm an art consultant," Joshua said.

"That doesn't answer my question," Leah returned.

"Mine either."

"Are you going to call Markov?" Leah asked.

Joshua raised a white-gloved hand and took a sip of his golden brown Miyabikyo. "He's not a man one wants to keeping waiting."

"Yet here you are, not giving into your wants."

Joshua looked at her. She had yet be this close to him, in this kind of light, gazing into this kind of stare. Cherries sunk in tubs of dark chocolate, bathing in syrup. Sad, sweet, intense, reserved—she read too much into them. His eyes were not Chihuly glassworks. There had been no artistic intent in their creation, right?

Or, maybe, God had taken some extra time with this one.

"Balance was Matisse's dream of art," Joshua said. "As art reflects life, I've come to believe balance is the key to everything. We learn it before our first birthdays. Getting up, tumbling, dropping, rising again, until finally we're waddling along—pushing our need to go against the limits of nature, ours and the world's. When that gets easy, we forget the first and most important lesson. Balance."

"Huh," Leah said. "Sounds like you thought about this."

"I was chained to a bed for thirty-six hours. It wasn't all romance. And my companion was balance-challenged, shall we say."

"You're sure you don't want to fill out a complaint?"

"There's no point," Joshua said. "She can't help it."

"As in mental disorder?"

"She is obsessive."

"That is beyond obsession. You and this woman have a history?"

Joshua sipped his whisky, taking his time. "Epic."

Leah took a healthy gulp of her own cocktail.

"I've got to call Stepan," Joshua took a phone out of his pocket. "I don't think this is one of those times when a text will do."

"I don't want you to mention your location," Leah said. "Find out what he wants with you."

"No offense, but this isn't exactly FBI business any longer."

"I'll decide that."

"What are you going to do if I disobey? Handcuff me to a bed-post?"

"I'll put you right back where I found you," Leah said.

"Fine." Joshua took the glove off his right hand and swished his thumb around the face of his phone. Then he put the phone up to his ear. "Hey," he said after two seconds. "Thank you for sending in the Feds." He paused, listening. Leah drank and watched his face. His eyes darted around, like he was trying to see what he imagined. It made him appear alert and concerned, which made Leah alert and concerned.

"I'll be right there." Joshua ended his call and looked at Leah. "I've got to go."

"To meet Markov."

"He was very insistent."

"I'm going with you."

"That's not necessary."

"Your comments aren't necessary," Leah said. "Sorry. That sounded less harsh in my head. You can comment all you want, I'm still coming with you."

"I will be fine, Special Agent Capello." Joshua returned his phone to his pocket and his glove to his hand.

"Ha." What started out as fake laugh turned into a real one. "We've met twice. Both times you were anything but fine."

Joshua shifted his lips to the left. His eyebrows fattened and sunk. "Those were . . . these have been special circumstances. It's not always like this. Besides, Stepan is a friend."

"He stole a painting to get my attention. Even billionaire oligarchs don't do that on a whim. He's as obsessive as Marisa and you didn't care for the way that worked out."

Joshua tossed some money on the bar. "There is not a 'plus one' on my invite."

"Let's try this another way," Leah said. "You want to get to Markov's fast and I've got a car with a siren. How's that sound?"

The car hadn't been moved or ticketed or booted. It was boxed in by a cab and a limo. Leah took out here badge and slapped it on the cab's windshield. She picked it up and flashed it in front of the limo and got in her sedan. Joshua got in the other side.

"Freakin' pros know the sedan is law enforcement," she said. "No respect. Now where am I going?"

Joshua gave her the address. Leah pulled out into traffic and sped uptown. No sirens.

"I respect the fact that you haven't asked about the gloves," Joshua said. "Most women do by now."

"I am not most women," Leah said. "My wondering about your fashion choices is taking a backseat to whether or not the Russian mob wants you dead."

CHAPTER SIX

Stepan Markov's apartment capped off an eighteen-floor building overlooking Central Park. Leah had seen the building before. At one point or another everyone in the City had wandered within eye-shot of it and said 'I wonder if God still lives there or got priced out of the place?' Lavish art deco darts and runs carried the eye up to the Hollywood version of an Egyptian temple on top, festooned with a topiary garden.

As they approached the front, Leah pegged the doorman as real New York. Mid-thirties, thin mustache, donning charcoal wool with gold piping. Very authentic. He had a disarming smile. The kind that never settles into a warm gaze. His body language and eye movements made him seem at once a concierge and special forces.

Which was fine with her. The foyer wouldn't smell like pee.

The doorman noticed them through glass that could've been used for a dolphin tank. He glanced down at the top of his standing desk. Leah couldn't see what he saw because of the privacy panel. He looked up again, resumed his professional smile and opened the door. He said proper good evenings as they entered and motioned them towards the elevators. He shot past them, and urged them to the last door. He waved a plastic card and opened that door too.

She would've cooed at the whole experience ten years ago. A doorman in stripped pants, a private elevator cast from one ton of brass, a building that had been around since people dressed like Monopoly pieces. Quintessential. Or iconic. If you were raised upstate and only experienced the City through camera lenses. After a decade, the glamor of New York had become chronic and she'd outgrown cooing.

The game hadn't change, though. Who owned what, lived where, and had the cash reserves to make your life miserable still rep-resented a score. Of sorts. Leah had, in the past, thought about how those games played out in a building like this one. You had to be terrifyingly wealthy to purchase a second floor apartment in the back. What did they think of someone who could swoop in and perch on the top floor? What did they think of a man who could steal a painting just to summon an agent of the FBI?

They would think he was dangerous.

"How long have you known Mr. Markov?" Leah asked.

"A couple of years," Joshua said into the elevator door.

"Two?"

"More like five," Joshua corrected. "But with him it's more about quality than quantity."

"Then there shouldn't be a problem," Leah returned.

"No."

"You trying to convince me or you?"

The private elevator space opened into a narrow, black and white tiled hall. It lacked the drama she had expected. She quickly figured out the hall was an architectural consent to having both a drool-worthy wrap around terrace, and allowing people access to it. It contained a mid-century chair, in gold mohair, draped with a very small, very red and blue windbreaker. Tiny sneakers lay nearby. Leah wished she were better with sizes. She could only decide on 'little'. She needed to know more about kids. She'd have to eventually. As per her sister, kids needed new shoes every seven or eight minutes, not someone telling them that their Rubens was a knock-off.

Markov's constant companion, Yuri, met Leah and Joshua at the door and directed them to the main living space. Two stories of windows set off the gleam of the city at night. Glowing steel and glass, standing around the black-green forest as if it were a model in the Museum of Natural History.

Leah refused to let the stun of the setting linger. She swept wide, so she could watch the bodyguard, Joshua and Markov at the same time. Yuri stood facing her, but at a distance. Behind him was a wall of photos. Different shapes and sizes, in a plethora of frames. Each picture showed a good amount of photographic talent. Most were of Markov and a little blond boy. Three had a woman, too. A blonde Christine Dior model, laughing and messing with the little guy's hair.

The center of the large, rectangular room had three rectangular sofas, set in U shape, allowing everyone a decent view. The room had a muted color palate. Soft greens, pale yellows, nothing strong enough to compete with the windows or, hanging on the far wall, what she believed to be a Chagall. An expansive work – she guessed six feet high – all misty primary colors depicting a rolling, romantic farm. She didn't recognize the piece, thank God. That meant it wasn't on her mental list of stolen paintings.

She unstuck her eyes to check out the young woman curled up on the end of the couch that faced her. Black print skirt and yellow blouse, shoes off. Handkerchief sagging in her hands. She might have been the woman from the photos on the wall. She had the right body for it. Tonight's face was not so photogenic. Eyes like red balloons, trailing strings of black mascara.

Markov stood just behind her, leaning on the back of the couch, still in the suit he'd had on at the gallery. The chipper blues and yellows didn't match the feel of the room. These two had not dressed for this occasion.

"Special Agent Capello," Markov said. "You did not have to deliver Joshua personally."

"I wanted to make sure he got here all safe and such."

"We thank you very much. Yuri will show you out."

"I'm in no hurry," Leah said.

"We don't want to take up any more of your time."

"It doesn't work like that." Leah walked farther into the room. "Did you ever hear the expression, 'the genie is out of the bottle'?"

"I am not so familiar with that one."

"You got me out of the bottle and made your wish. Getting me back in is a whole 'nother story."

"We have urgent business, Joshua and me."

Leah sat down across from the woman. She knew her look, not the reason. This fit and prim mid-thirties blond—her whole job as a billionaire's wife could be summed up thus: Poise. Boring functions, sleepy concerts, barbed dinners and prickly event—she had to keep it together. Right now, she could not. Her lips quaked when Leah looked at her. The saline output from her eyes rose by 30-percent.

"Hi," Leah said. "I don't believe we've met."

The woman had an expression for which Leah had no name. A woman on a sinking ship, staring at you in your seaworthy lifeboat. Like that painting, *The Raft of the Medusa*. Anguish and anger.

She looked up at Markov, who patted her shoulder.

"It is now time to leave," Markov said.

"Are you OK?" Leah asked the woman.

She pressed her lips together with enough force to make them vanish.

"Go!" Markov barked. "I have not enough time for this shit!"

Yuri took a step towards Leah, approaching from the left.

"Stepan." Joshua walked over to the window. "The agent is in no hurry to go anywhere. The hurry is all yours."

"I will not have this in my house!" Markov said.

Yuri moved closer. Leah adjusted her position on the couch so she could quickly draw her weapon. Again. What was it with these the people? She bent her head towards the woman across from her, keeping her eyes on the big Russian with the concealed firearm. Probably fire-arms. Plural. And a push knife. He seemed the type.

"Ma'am," Leah said. "How about you and I go outside? Get a little fresh air."

"This is troubling me," Markov said. "I think I am having to call your *bobyshka*."

He was losing his excellent English, Leah realized. Not cool.

"I can't leave you here in obvious distress," Leah said to the woman. "Hell, I won't leave Joshua either because there is something not right here. Really, truly not right. There's been some shouting. Why don't you go check on your son?"

"I can't." The woman's face cracked.

"Lidiya!" Markov spat.

Leah felt her stomach crush in on itself. "Where's your little boy, ma'am?"

The woman didn't answer. Leah guessed she didn't have one.

CHAPTER SEVEN

Leah watched as Stepan Markov placed his hands on the back of the couch, just behind Lidiya's shoulders, and braced his arms. He lowered his head as she raised hers and their foreheads touched. They stayed that way for a while. Leah had no desire to break the spell.

"I don't think it's going to work," Joshua said with a therapist's tone.

"We have his jacket," Markov said. "We should try."

"I've got to call this in," Leah cut in.

"You can't." Markov brought up his head to address Leah. Lidiya lowered hers. "They were very clear about not involving police."

"They always are," Leah returned. "They don't want to face the full power of the Bureau."

"This is not the common kidnapping," Markov countered. "The people who took my little boy are not waiting for a sack of money. If I follow their instructions, my boy will be returned."

"Start at the beginning, please," Leah said.

"Where's the jacket?" Joshua interjected.

Markov glanced at Yuri and nodded. Yuri started back towards the entrance hall.

"No," Joshua said. "Take me to it. The fewer people who touch it the better."

Leah stood. She needed to plant her feet. Take a few deep breaths. Training, instincts, common sense and compassion pulled her in different directions. Yuri motioned for Joshua to follow him back down the hall. Towards that toddler jacket on the mid-century chair, she figured. Markov squeezed Lidiya's shoulders as she patted his hands.

A flood of questions rushed over Leah. She had to pick something, grab on and pull herself out of this swirl. She didn't understand Joshua's bit in all this, so screw it. Contacting the office would really bring the shit. She picked, *Help the boy.* Which meant calling in the kidnapping squad, which she could do five minutes from now just as easily as she could right now.

"When was your son taken?" she asked.

"Around eleven this morning," Lidiya answered. "We were at the park."

"There must have been witnesses."

"They made it look not like a kidnapping. The kidnappers. No one saw a thing."

"Did you have anyone with you?"

"We have a man for when we go out."

"Where is he?"

"Home," Lidiya said. "He is getting better."

"Was there a struggle?"

"I wish," Markov said. "Boris would have won in a fight."

"There was a dog," Lidiya continued. "A pretty dog and a pretty woman walking this dog. Stepan Jr. played on a slide and this dog bit at our man, Boris. He tried to be nice. Not to shoot this dog in a playground full of children. This woman pretends to be nice and the dog attacks again. I get up to go to him and I bump this man with his latte and we are a mess. The two of us. Boris kicks this dog and everyone is now grabbing for their children. I go to the slide and I see . . . the jacket. Stepan is not with his jacket. I run and I look and . . ."

Leah let her trail off. She wanted more details, more story, more to work with – more, more, more than the mom could give right now.

"The jacket had a note," Markov said.

"May I see it?" Leah asked.

Markov walked under the second-story wall, the one with the Chagall. Leah turned at the hips, to the sound of Joshua and Yuri returning. Joshua carried the red and blue jacket. He set it on the arm as if it were cashmere and sat down angled towards Lidiya. He folded his white-gloved hands in his lap.

"I didn't get anything off the coat," he said. "That is actually good news. Nothing traumatic happened to little Stepan while he wore it."

"What do you mean?" Leah asked. "You dusted and ran prints? Plucked hair-strands? What are you talking about?"

Markov crossed the living room, carrying a standard sheet of white paper, folded in thirds. "I appreciate you trying. I know you are not a hound."

"You sniffed the jacket?" Leah felt her lip curl on the left side. She smoothed it before anyone saw indignation.

As Markov passed between the sofas, Joshua leapt up. He spread his hands around the paper, a magician about to change it into a dove. "Is this a note from the captors?"

"Yes, I—"

"May I?"

Markov moved the sheet into his hands. Joshua put his left hand to his mouth and pulled its glove off with his teeth. He pressed the paper between his two hands, like he was going to say an oath on it, Leah might have thought, had he not done something very similar to the painting, in that hotel room, back when they had first met. He closed his eyes. His lips pursed and pulsed with in such a minute motion no one would notice, unless they were staring, hard, at his plump, pumping lips.

He opened his eyes. Everyone watched, rapt, as he shook his head.

"Machines," Joshua said. "They leave nothing. I am so sorry." He made a controlled collapse into the couch, next to Leah. She bent over and slipped the note from his hands and read—

STAY HOME TOMORROW NIGHT AND YOUR SON WILL BE RETURNED TO YOU. TELL NO ONE.

Leah put her full focus on Markov. "What do they mean?"

"Thank you for being so understanding," he returned.

"Why do you think they want you here tomorrow night?"

"I'm putting my wife to bed. She has had a difficult day."

"It is time to call in the experts. Trust me, the FBI has trained professionals. People who do this all the time."

"So do I." Markov's voice sounded like a stone dropped into a creek. "I mean you and your FBI no disrespect. I have some experience in these matters. If you call your comrades, I will tell them that little Stepan is with his grandmother and you are harassing my wife and I for reasons we do not understand. You will protest and it will be for nothing. My boy will be back to us before you convince anyone that anything is wrong. You go, Special Agent Capello. You do what you feel you need to do. We will do the same."

"I—"

Joshua took her wrist. He held it through his gloved hand as he got up from the couch. "Lidiya, Stepan," he said, "if there is anything else we can do, just call. I will not let my phone get too far from me until this is all over."

As the Markovs gave their thank-yous Joshua dragged Leah out. She could've flipped him and cuffed him before he knew he'd made a mistake. Damn right, she could have. And should have.

She would have, had she been certain he'd made a mistake.

CHAPTER EIGHT

"You can let go now," Leah said as the elevator doors closed. Joshua let go of her wrist and she faced him, not the door. She said, "Talk," and nothing else.

"Talk about what?" Joshua stayed facing forward.

She stared into the side of his face.

Joshua said, "You said 'talk' and left out the subject."

Leah didn't know this guy that well. At all, really. She did not consider herself particularly proficient at nonverbal communication. She had been recruited by the Bureau for her skills with the symbolic forms of communication. Yet, she could tell the silent treatment wormed its way into him.

He squirmed. "I can talk about all kinds of things," he said. "Early Renaissance frescoes? American Abstract Expressionism? My early childhood, skipping rocks down by the 'ole swimming hole? What do you want?"

The elevator settled and the doors parted. They exited into more brass and marble, headed for the oversized deco doors.

"I was a happy kid, with lots of friends and family."

The doorman saw them in corner of his eye and opened the doors as they approached.

"I had a dog named Champ and a cat named Whiskers, a loving but stern father who spent too much time down at the plant, and a mother who baked cookies every afternoon."

Leah crossed behind Joshua as they approached her black sedan. He reached for the handle of the front passenger door. She reached passed him, and opened the rear door.

"You've got to be kidding."

Leah reached up to press his head down, to make sure he didn't bump it on his way in.

"No, no," he protested. "I've got it." He cringed and rolled into the backseat before she got a hand on him, escaping her touch. Just like the hotel room.

Leah rounded the car, hopped in and sat. She didn't bother turning over the engine. Her stomach turned enough for the car and both people in it. Kidnapping. A little boy. Walking away from an active crime.

One summer, years ago, when she was around ten or so, she and her sister spent a week with their grandparents at their cabin upstate. The woods were fun. Except one night she chased a firefly off the path and got confused. She stood alone, in the forest, at night, with no clue whether to go left or right or anything in between. She had no path.

Eventually she decided on yelling. She yelled and yelled until her sister came and got her. She wanted to yell now. Not for her sister. She simply wanted to yell and yell and yell. She put her back to the door, legs up on the seat, and peered at Joshua through the plastic mesh keeping passengers from bothering anyone in the front.

"AAAAAAAA," she screamed at him.

"Yeah," Joshua replied. "There's a lot of that going around."

"And you're freakin' patient zero."

"Can you take me to my apartment?"

"This isn't a car service."

"I know who pinned that note the Stepan Jr.'s jacket."

"And you're just telling me now? And you didn't tell Markov? And you think that's going to get you to your apartment? It's getting you into an interrogation room. Downtown. With a bare light bulb and everything. No, maybe . . . with touching. I'm going to cuff you to the table and touch your cheeks. Oh God. I just remembered you like that. That's how I freakin' found you. Son of a . . . How do you know who pinned the note?"

"I just do," Joshua said.

"Wrong answer," Leah said. "A little boy is in trouble and you're giving me that crap?"

"It's compli—"

"If you say 'complicated,' I'm going to shoot you in the foot. Do you understand me? It will hurt now and for the rest of you life, so do not say 'complicated'. That's what people say to those they think are either stupid or can't handle the truth. While I am not always the brightest bulb on the string—as evidenced by the fact that I am sitting here with you—I am not technically stupid. On the matter of truth, it is my *raison d'être*. It is why I joined the Bureau and also why I am sitting here with you. So. How do you know who pinned that note?"

Joshua sat back in the rear seat. Leah could only see parts of him through the mesh and shadows. He put his hands behind his head, pushed air out through his mouth and gazed through the window, through the spotty traffic, into the deep darkness of Central Park. Lights from passing cars shimmered across his eyes. Bright bulbs, Leah thought. Eyes too bright on a man too charming.

"The 'how' is not important," Joshua said.

"Provenance is always important," Leah returned in an even voice. "You should know that better than anyone. Isn't that how you earn a living? Verifying the provenance of art works? Making sure they are what the seller claims?"

"In this case, the history isn't important."

"Intelligence gathering is also based on provenance," Leah said. "The number of sources, the quality of sources—it all matters, from spying to Times reporting to Kosher beef." Leah spun on her seat and reached for the car's start button. "I think we'll talk better down at One Federal Plaza. I don't need Markov's permission to file a missing persons report."

"That night we first met," Joshua started. "At the hotel. If it had been just Markov, Allen and myself things would've gone better. The sale still would have collapsed—Allen brought a forgery, after all—the sale would have collapsed and we would have all parted peacefully. No knives, no guns, no one in jail. But . . ."

"But the FBI was there."

"You are disruptive. Not just because you're the feds. Any third party in that room might have cranked up the nonsense. I've been part of a great deal of deals. The fewer parties involved, the more likely they are to run smoothly. This business with Stepan Jr. is a deal."

"A big deal," Leah said. "Which is why we need help."

"You don't want these people who took little Stepan to start erasing their tracks. You understand the first track they will erase."

First, kill the boy. That's what they'd have to do. Leah grabbed the steering wheel with both hands and began an attempt to pry it from the steering column. After the pain in her wrists and arms and shoulders built to the point of distraction she stopped and sat back.

"Who pinned that note?" she asked.

"I don't know her name," Joshua replied.

"What do you know?"

"Her face."

"You saw a woman pin a note to a kidnap victim's jacket?"

"Yes."

"You were there?"

"No."

"You what?" Leah asked. "You saw it on YouTube?"

"Let me rephrase," Joshua said. "I have an idea as to who one of the kidnappers might be. I don't have a name but I know who might."

"That's all you got?"

"That's it."

Leah pushed the red 'start' button and looked into the rearview mirror, at her passenger. "I'm going to find these guys and offer them a trade. The boy for you."

CHAPTER NINE

Joshua Fawls made several phone calls as Leah drove back downtown. She tried to listen in. The single words, lack of proper nouns and complete absence of context left her with very little. He seemed to be looking for somebody named Scott and insisting on finding him now. At least she agreed with him on something.

Time had special qualities in abduction cases. It was at once too short and interminably long.

Leah had not contemplated abductions since Quantico, thankfully. She had seen their lasting effect on her instructors. When they talked about kidnappings, they never fully spoke from the past, even when the cases were decades old. Abductions had a pernicious, persistent quality. In the abductee, the crime created its own witness. Criminals tended not to care for witnesses. In the wait for the payoff, the crime created its own ticking clock. The crime gave those involved time to act, gather evidence, solve. The chance is always limited, flimsy and, in the end, cruel. Kidnappings gave you opportunity, no matter how small and rigged. The crime gave you the chance to get things right or to roll it over in your head for the rest of your life.

The stop and go of the city inched tonight. Glaring red lights at every corner, double parked trucks, cones, cranes, kids walking backwards while they joked with their forward-walking buddies, too happy and goofy and young to watch for angry black sedans.

In grad school Leah had been shown a painting brought to the University for an opinion. The owner believed it to be a Jackson Pollock. A drip painting, big, bold and broad. Thousands of squiggly lines. Leah had seen real Pollocks. Crazy random messes that somehow compelled you to look deeper, harder, coaxing you to complete the work, to make the final connections between the art and the meaning. This painting had all the random craziness and nothing else. On instinct, she knew the painting was a fake. It just wasn't right.

Like this kidnapping. She had no doubt that the child had been taken. She had no doubt that the Markovs were under duress. She doubted everything else. Starting with the passenger—suspect—conman—partner in the back.

She waited for him to end his fourth call, and asked, "Why didn't you tell Markov you knew something?"

"I'm not sure what I know matters," Joshua replied.

"You held out on him," Leah said. "When he learns this, he's not going to like it and I have the sense that he won't bottle it up until he can share it with his therapist."

"That would be progress."

"Explain the risk-reward ratio here," Leah demanded.

Joshua put down his phone and leaned up close to the plastic fencing running between the back and front seats. "There are many ways to skin a cat. With Stepan, it is usually a hammer and spike. If I had told him what I know . . . there would be messes to clean up."

Why did she ever ask this guy a question? Why?

"What's tomorrow night?" she asked, despite herself. Despite knowing full well he'd supply another hollow, useless answer.

"Thursday," Joshua said. "Mmmm. Meatloaf, I think."

"Yeah," Leah replied. "See, answers like that are the reason we invented enhanced interrogation techniques. Every time you speak, I'm thinking I could totally waterboard you. Thirty years of Catholic upbringing? Bonus. I'm going old school on your ass. I'm Googling plans for a rack."

"The best torture devices are in the vaults of the Vatican. Leftovers from their more inquisitive years."

"The ransom note told Markov to stay home tomorrow night. Stay home from what?"

"I don't know," Joshua said. "I honestly don't know."

Joshua's face softened slightly. To Leah, it looked like he wanted to know. Like he should know.

"Stepan texted me a while back," Joshua continued. "He asked if I would be in town tomorrow night. I said yes and he asked me – told me, really—to keep my calendar open. That was all. No what, where or when."

"This is the place?" Leah slowed the car, edging towards the right.

"That's what they said." Joshua hunched to see out the front windshield. The sign running up the corner of the building read TIGHT. Black and white posters in the upper windows showed incredibly fit men and woman twisting and bending and straining against bars and ropes.

Leah parked the car in the space warned off by a fire hydrant. She got out, looked up at the place, rolled her eyes, walked around the car and opened the back door like a chauffeur.

"We've arrive at your destination, sir," she said as Joshua emerged.

"Excellent," he returned. "If I'm not out in a hour, it means I've hooked up with a yoga instructor and you can take the car home."

"Is Scott here?" Leah asked.

Joshua pumped his eyebrows once.

"Scott," Leah continued. "I heard you mention him on the phone."

"Asuna is here," Joshua answered.

"Who the crap is that?"

"She may know where we can find Scott. She's not answering her phone. I can only guess as to why."

Leah started towards the front door. Joshua passed her and spun. "I was serious about you waiting."

"Or you could be silly about me waiting. I don't care either way." Leah continued walking, forcing Joshua to shift left or be touched. God forbid she brush up against him. How did he live in this city? You can't go two blocks on this island without someone bumping you. "What does Asuna look like?"

"She's going to know you're a cop."

"Then she'll be wrong. I'm not a cop."

They walked through the front door of the gym. They couldn't get any father than the vestibule without a valid membership card to swipe.

"It is the wrong time to try to persuade our way in," Leah said. "Not too many people coming and going. We could be here a while."

"This won't take long." Joshua popped open a small door on the card reader. It hid a small keypad. He took off his right glove and gently placed his spread hand across the keys.

"You know the code?"

"Shush," he said and closed his eyes.

Leah stood straight. She felt the back of her neck redden. Nobody shu—

Joshua put his glove back on and pressed six keys. The light on top of the card reader turned green and she heard the deadbolt with-draw.

"What?" came out of her mouth.

"Later." Joshua pushed open the door and held it for her.

They strolled through the gym, sparsely populated, but still more people than Leah expected this close to 11 on a weeknight. The designers had left lots of exposed brick and accented it with chrome and steel. The artificial scent of fresh linen flowed through the place. A pleasant disguise for the smell of antiseptics fighting bacteria.

Two people rode stationary bikes. Neither one of them could have been called Asuna under any circumstance. Leah and Joshua continued through the heard of treadmills and stair machines and stopped.

Shiny black and lime green Lycra, inky razor-cut hair, a 5'2" protein supplement spokesperson bounced around in the far corner. She worked a heavy bag, kicking and punching to a rhythm Leah couldn't hear. She understood it, though. Burn calories and tone muscle while doing routine that didn't feel like a complete waste of time. She did a similar workout herself, every other . . . regularly . . . she needed to get back at that. French, playing the flute, self-defense skills: use them or lose them.

The woman stopped and spun before Leah and Joshua got within three strides. She yanked out her earbuds. Leah wanted to know how she knew they approached. What a great skill to have.

"Asuna." Joshua clasped his hands behind his back. He put out a smile so wide and sparkling Leah felt one grow across her own lips.

The woman said nothing. She stood with her legs and arms bent. Ready. Leah decided to go the opposite way. Sometimes a scene needed contrast to balance out. She cocked out a hip, folded her arms and looked around like she couldn't give two shits.

"I got your name from Pete," Joshua said. "Dominican Pete."

"Dominican Pete would've told you I don't take walk ups." The woman Leah now guessed was Asuna said. "You need to make an appointment."

"I'm looking for Scott."

"Scott who?"

Joshua lowered his head and glared at the woman. "Scott."

The woman glared back. "I'm gonna finish my reps now, K?"

"Two weeks ago," Joshua said, "I authenticated a Calder mobile for Winston Parr. Do you know Winston Parr? Anyway, he's producing *Wonder Woman the Musical*. Soon his search will begin for perfect Amazonian warriors."

Asuna dropped her head and let it swing back and forth a few times.

"I didn't charge him," Joshua said. "I don't charge friends."

Asuna picked her head up and looked Leah up and down. Leah looked right back, tapping her foot. Then looked away again, trying to seem impatient and uninterested.

"What kind of production? Off, Off Broadway or what?"

"I don't know where he's going to start it, but we're talking Winston Parr. After tweaking, it's eight shows a week, whining about ticket scalpers and when are the Tonys."

"Scott's at Brozilla. On 9th. You know it?"

"They serve an exquisite Linzer tart."

Asuan smirked. "That's the place. You forward my number to Parr."

"I'll write it on his bathroom wall."

Asuna whirled and kicked the bag. Hard.

Leah turned before she looked impressed.

CHAPTER TEN

The gym and Brozilla were too close. Leah didn't have time to assail Joshua with the eighty-three new questions she'd come up with. A sliver of a place, blacked out down to the doorknobs. Had she ever stumbled across this place she never would have gone in. She pulled the car up next to a row of motorcycles, five long. Leather and chrome. Mostly leather.

"Are you going to tell me to sit this one out?" Leah asked as they neared the door.

"You still have your gun?"

"Because I will. I'll wait right here for . . . what did you say? An hour? I don't know if there are too many yoga instructors in there. I'm betting you could hook up, though."

They walked in. The club could not have been eight feet wide. Black on black on black. Tiny ceiling lights reflected off the mirrors behind the bar. Flashes of white scurried around the place, refracting through glasses and bottles. None of it was enough to brighten the place. Dance music thumped. Not so loud that it hurt. Four men sat at the bar, representing at least a half-ton of mass. Not counting the chains and studs.

Each looked over their shoulders as Leah and Joshua entered. None of them lingered on Leah. They watched Joshua like he was the ice cream truck. In July.

Leah hung back and let Joshua step up to the bar. She peered into the square black hole that made up the back of the bar. A faint hall, then stairwells going up and down.

"What can I get you?" The bartender asked. 5'10", 175, black leather vest doing nothing for his arms. Black goatee doing nothing for his face.

"Scott," Joshua said. "You can get me Scott."

"And you think Scott wants to be got?"

Joshua reached in his back pocket and slid out a slim fold of bills. His white gloves glowed in the bar lights. They were the brightest things in the place. He put a hundred dollar bill on the bar. "Two bourbons. Your choice."

The bartender paused long enough to make a point, then reached under the bar for two rocks glasses. Leah checked the entrance again. Clear exit. She checked the back. Nothing. She moved closer to Joshua as the bartender filled the glasses with brown liquid from a bottle she didn't recognize. Bottom shelf bourbon. Was it worth it? Was she on duty? Was this drink pretty much medicinal at this point?

Joshua handed her the glass as he picked up his own. He clinked hers as she took it.

"Cheers," he said.

She threw the whole shot back.

Joshua sipped his. "This feels like a second date."

"You obviously don't have a girlfriend."

The bartended played his phone with both thumbs. Leah guessed he sent a text.

"I'm exploring my options," Joshua said. "And you?"

"Every time I meet someone interesting, they turn out to have more issues than National Geographic. Know what I'm saying?"

"I would've thought there were lots fish in your office pond."

"Where I work, the cute ones tend to be on their way to Attica."

Joshua grinned. The bartender looked up from his phone.

"You can head down," he said.

Leah led the way. She had no strong desire to descend the stairs. The situation reminded her of drills back at Quantico. Targets popping up, swinging in, pushing your blood into such a rush you think your ears are going to burst. These were not great memories. As this was not a great situation.

The stairs leveled out into a hallway, with doors right, left and forward. The only light came from a tube of blue mini bulbs, casting just enough to keep you from busting your nose on a wall. The door at the end was the only one open. A flicker of orangey-yellow glow seeped out.

She approached with caution. She did not want to go through. The dark, the narrow access, the complete unknown on the other side. She could send Joshua through first. That would have been the smart thing to do. Of course, she didn't do things that way. Not tonight.

"This way," came a male voice from the side and two steps back. "Don't be shy." The side door. Someone inside had wanted to watch them pass before making their presence known. That was reason enough not to enter.

Kidnapping, Leah said to herself. *A little boy. You can suck this up, girl. Get through the door.*

Leah pushed open the door and entered the room. Five pillar candles burned on an end table in the left corner, not more than ten feet away. Red sectional couches lined the left wall and wall across from the entrance. A man sat next to the candles, jeans, white T-shirt, legs crossed giving her a good view of his enormous black combat boots. Not that she considered them for too long. The satin fish concealing his entire head compelled her attention.

"Come all the way in, please," came through the fish's mouth. A theatrical mask. Elaborate.

A rustle on her right.

"Try not to move," fishhead said.

She ignored him, darting her head in the direction of the sound. A second man, in jeans and black T-shirt, with another shimmering fish mask. Bright yellow, red, blue and orange. This time it was the shotgun that drew her eyes. Fishhead number two had it aimed at her midsection.

"Alright, let's try that again," the first fishhead said. "Don't move."

CHAPTER ELEVEN

"What do you want with Scott?" asked the man on the red couch, the fish-puppet thing covering his entire head.

Leah kept her eyes on the other fishheaded man. The one with the shotgun, dull steel and wood and too long for the room. A field gun. She positioned herself to keep Joshua from coming any farther into the room.

"I—" Joshua started.

Leah cut him off. "Put the gun down."

"We ask the questions," fishhead number two said. "Answers first." His voice had lots of snarl. Too much, really.

"How about some civility first," Leah returned.

"How 'bout you talk." He stood flat to them, with the butt of the weapon against his side. Against his side? Nothing behind it but air? This fish had never fired a firearm in his life.

"Tell us what you want with Scott," the original fishhead said. "And we can all walk away from this."

The range of vision in that stupid headgear must have been next to nothing. They had to look out through mouths.

Joshua said, "We just want to—"

Leah grabbed the shotgun, shoved it to her left, aiming it in the direction of the fishhead on the couch. The gun-fish did not pull the trigger. The attack left Leah's arm across her body. Terrible form. Awkward. She had one good option. She kneed fishhead number two in the crotch. Fast. The man screamed and doubled over. Leah wrenched the shotgun from his hands and used the butt to push him to the ground as she moved behind him.

"I did not see that coming," Joshua said.

"Stay down," Leah said to the man on the ground. She looked at the man on the couch, balled up like a potato bug. "And you. Take off the fish before I . . . before I fry it."

"You could have gone with fillet," Joshua said.

"You are not helping," Leah said. Her heart pumped hard. She was glad the room was so dark. She didn't want these guys seeing her chest heaving. The man on the couch pulled the mask off his head and shook out his dirt brown hair. She glanced at the gun in her hands. Scroll work on the sides. An under-over, if she remembered correctly. She was no expert. The weapon had style, though. Over-the-mantle style.

"Are you Scott?" Joshua asked the man on the couch.

"Who wants to know?"

"Was that your audition for *Law and Order?*" Joshua asked. "Because it could use some work."

The man tipped his head back, defiant. "Who wants to know?" he delivered with a sneer.

"Better," Joshua said.

"Cut the crap," Leah said. "Are you Scott or not?"

"Yeah, yeah," Scott said.

"Can I take my mask off, too?" the man on the floor asked.

"No," Leah answered.

"Scott," Joshua continued. "We're looking for a woman on your crew."

"I don't know what you're talking about."

"A redhead. Freckles. You know who I mean."

"You got the wrong guy."

"Look, Scott and Scott's friend," Joshua said. "Two weeks ago I authenticated a Calder mobile for Winston Parr. You know him, right? The producer with more Tony's than Trattoria's on a Friday night? He told me about his new project. *Wonder Woman the Musical.*"

"That's why you want Dani?" Scott sprang wide and exhaled.

Finally, Leah said inside. *A name.*

"I need to get in touch with her," Joshua said.

"When are auditions?" the man on the floor asked.

"Can you get ahold of her?" Joshua continued.

"Sure, sure." Scott sat, trying to relax.

The man on the floor asked, "Can I take this off now?"

"No," Leah said.

"It's hot."

"No it's not. Trust me."

"How did they dance in these things?" he called out.

"They didn't," Scott returned. "That's why they got tossed."

"I was thinking you'd call her now," Joshua said.

"Like, right now?" Scott asked. "It's, like, 11:30?"

"Text her," Joshua said. "Ask her where she is."

"What's the rush? It's not like there are auditions tonight, right?"

"There are going to be no auditions for you unless I'm talking to Dani by midnight."

Scott reached behind him. Leah raised the long gun. Scott pulled out his phone and started dabbing away at it.

Leah cracked open the shotgun barrels at the breach and withdrew its two cartridges from their respective chambers. "This is the nicest gun I've ever held."

"Thanks," the man on the floor said. "It was my grandfather's."

"This wasn't here, in the bar, for emergencies, was it?"

"A bar gun?" The man on the floor sounded incensed. "Hardly."

"I'm thinking you don't just walk around with a treasure like this. Even if you are coming to Brozilla. You grabbed it so you could set this trap."

"We were being cautious," the man said.

"Why so cautious?" She dropped the cartridges into her jacket pocket. They didn't fit well. Jumbo Chapsticks, destroying the lie of the fabric near her hip.

"We don't know you," he said.

"Get up." Leah snapped the shotgun back together.

"Thank God." The man on the floor scurried to a stand.

"Take that stupid-ass fishhead off and sit yourself next to your pal."

"Sassy," he said as he lifted the headpiece off.

"I've got the gun."

"She's not answering," Scott said. "She's probably asleep."

The man from the floor had curly black hair and a broad face. five-eleven, and looked like a hundred-fifty pounds. Leah raised her guess fifteen pounds based on muscle mass. Twenty-five years at the oldest, the man had deep contours. Thick legs.

"Are you a dancer?" she asked.

"Singer and actor, too" He sat next to Scott.

"What's your name, triple threat?"

"Van."

Joshua sat down on red couch that ran perpendicular to one with Scott and Van. Leah closed the door. It had no effect on the lighting. That came from the fiery glow of the pillar candles on the end table at the junction of the couches. She realized now they were artificial. What a stupid ass room, with stupid ass masks and tasteless furniture and why would a freakin' bar even have a room like this?

"Which one of you did Asuna call?"

Scott and Van looked at each other. Then Scott nodded.

"She told you we were looking for you and your first instinct is to grab a shotgun and a couple of Mardi Gras masks?"

"We do a *Finding Nemo* bit—"

"Whatever." Leah cut him off. "That's pretty God damn jumpy. Why are you so paranoid?"

Scott and Van looked at each other again. They wanted to exchange information. Leah could tell they didn't agree. They hadn't thought any of this through.

"Where's Dani?" Leah demanded.

"I don't know," Scott answered. "Probably home."

"Where's home?"

"She's got a place in Brooklyn."

"God, really?"

"What? You thought she could afford this neighborhood?"

Leah leaned the shotgun against the wall. "I just didn't feel like driving any more."

"OK, boys." Joshua stood. "Let's take a ride."

"We're good," Scott said.

"Yeah," Van added. "I've had enough for tonight. My balls are killing me."

"We are pretending to be polite." Joshua picked up the shotgun. He held it up to get a good look at the scrollwork on the receiver.

"Seriously," Van said. "Nobody needs to see Dani this bad."

"We do," Leah said. "And you're coming with us."

Joshua kissed the side of the shotgun and leaned it back against the wall. Leah opened her mouth to say 'what the—'

Van cut her off. "I'm done with the diva bit, honey."

"It's played out." Scott added.

"You're both welcome to come." Leah drew her sidearm. She held it pointed up and snapped the slide for a nice, dramatic click. "Truth is, I only need one."

CHAPTER TWELVE

Leah and Joshua sat in the front, next to a short stack of phones that belonged to the young men in back. Scott and Van sat quietly as they all proceeded east towards the Queens-Midtown Tunnel, which Leah hated, because it was a tunnel—dark, ugly, a measly two openings, with a billion tons of water on top—and it had a toll. The car had an E-ZPass, so she didn't have to dig around in her pockets for cash, or worse, ask her new suspect-conman-partner to borrow a couple of bucks. She did have to contend with the records E-ZPasses produced. Signing out a car was one thing. Going to Brooklyn was something else altogether. It raised legitimate questions. First, by her. Like, when exactly did you lose all sense, girl?

"Joshua," Leah announced. "It's story time."

He glanced at her, all faux-sleepy, with lights striping his face and fading and re-striping as they moved through the city.

"Don't even," she said.

Joshua made one, slow blink. "Even if I promise to tell you everything someday, when I've got the energy?"

"That day is tonight."

"You're mixing your metaphors."

"That's how I roll. Bustin' names and takin' heads."

"Fine," he huffed. "These gentlemen are part of the Modigliani Gang."

"Whoa, dude," Van blurted.

"Where did you get that?" Scott's voice rose a full octave.

"You're shitting me," Leah said.

"I shit you not," Joshua replied. "Scott, Van, Dani and Asuna lifted *Nude Sitting on a Divan* from the home of Oscar Pierce, who had purchased it just a few weeks prior for $80 million. Making this the greatest, most daring art theft of the 21st century."

"Maybe of all time," Van added.

"It's debatable," Joshua said.

"These guys?" Leah drove. "The fishheads?"

"I don't know where you're getting your information," Scott said. "But you are way, way, way off. We are just a couple of guys trying to catch our break."

"Is there a better pool of potential art thieves?" Joshua proposed.

"These guys do not look like they're living the life," Leah said.

"That's what makes the story true," Joshua continued. "Nobody can fence Modigliani's *Nude*, right? The crime got an over abundance of press. In one of the great ironies of the art world, the painting went from $80 million to liability in about two minutes. The only way a crime like this makes sense is if the painting isn't really the goal."

"I don't know," Leah said. "$80 million pretty much seems like a goal."

"No," Joshua said. "The taking is the thing. Isn't that right, boys?"

"We don't know what you're talking about," Scott said.

"For some people, art is worth loving," Joshua said. "They see a painting like Modigliani's *Nude* and they have to have it. Other people want a painting simply because other people want the painting. Its value comes not from their own desire, but other people's desires."

"I know the type," Leah agreed.

"Then you know these kinds of people, the ones that live to out spend, out show, out life-style others. They can be very wealthy."

"I had your friend Stepan classified as one of those."

"He's more complex," Joshua said. "But he has that trait. It is, however, another man with that trait that hired this improv troupe. What are you called?"

"Boss Level Creatures," Van said.

"What?" Leah looked like she wanted to spit.

"This man was out-bid for the Modigliani," Joshua continued. "He and Oscar Pierce were frequent rivals. This time he couldn't leave it at auction house."

A rival of Oscar Pierce. Leah would know the man. She'd probably met him at one event or another. *Another time*, she chided herself. Stick to one crime at a time.

"He decided to steal the painting," Joshua said. "He didn't care about the money. His sole goal was making sure Pierce didn't have it. That's why the painting has never surfaced. No ransom has ever been asked. It's in the back of a closet in Midtown where it will stay until this man dies."

"You could join our troupe," Scott said. "You are very good at making stuff up."

"And so are you," Joshua replied. "Posing as the catering staff, creating a distraction with a lovers' quarrel culminating in a flaming ice sculpture—genius. A flaming ice sculpture! Pure genius."

"Is this the reason you nabbed us?" Van asked.

"I don't think so," Leah answered.

"Does it bother you?" Joshua softened his voice. "Your crime is world famous and you are not. You've obviously got talent. The theft was performance art the likes of which the world has never seen. Were I the performer, I think it would eat at me everyday. The misallocation of fame."

"Banksy does alright," Scott said.

"Perhaps. We don't really know, do we? He might think everyday the gimmick of secrecy is half the appeal of the art. He might wish he'd shown his face to the public right at the start so the art could be judged on it on its own, not as part of some global mystery game.

"Having remarkable talent and being forced to keep it back-stage, behind the curtain, it's not an aspiration of an artist. Art is about getting at the truth, not living a lie."

"We all live lies." Scott gazed out the window

"Some of us more than others." Leah looked at Joshua. "From Dani to these chumps to the Modigliani theft, you claim to know a lot of things you shouldn't. Or couldn't."

One of the phones in the stack chirped.

"See who it is," Leah said to Joshua.

He picked up one of the phones and said, "Asuna."

"She wants to know if her friends are all right. Hold up the phone." Leah angled her head towards the back. "Who's phone?"

Nothing.

"Come on now," Leah said. "We've gone this far together. There's no sense in making Asuna all worried."

"It's mine," Scott said.

"Give us the password and Joshua here will text her back that everything is wonderful."

"But it's not," Van said.

"But it's not bad, either."

Leah waited. She didn't want to start threatening these men again. They might harden. She felt close to hardening herself. The adrenaline released by her skirmish with Van had worn off about four blocks back.

"Scott," Leah said. "There's nothing to be gained from letting her pace back and forth until we're through with you."

"What's that supposed to mean?"

Leah sighed. "All I want is a quick chat with Dani. To see if my friend here is full of crap or full of shit. I can't decide. Dani will know."

"And then?"

Joshua had his gloves off and across his upper thigh. He pressed the phone between his hands and closed his eyes. A preacher, at a tent revival, forcing the demons out.

"What are you doing?" Leah demanded. "Seriously. I've seen you praying over things like three times now and it's really starting to bug me."

"God forbid I bug you." Joshua set the phone in his lap and picked up his gloves. "Though to be honest, I don't remember asking you to tag along on my little escapade."

"Tag along?" Leah said. "I'm the one driving. I'm driving this whole clusterpalooza and don't forget it. I'm not your little sister following you around the neighborhood, OK?"

Joshua poked his hands back into his gloves. "Only a little sister would say that." He picked up the phone.

"Scott," Leah called into the back. "Password. Now. Before we get to the tunnel."

"No need." Joshua tapped the phone. 1123. Leah could see the screen change. It let him in.

"Are you some kind of hacker, too?" she asked.

"I'm good at guessing passwords." Joshua typed a text message.

"You got into my phone?" Scott exclaimed.

"I am sorry," Joshua replied. "I'm not looking through your browser history. Just telling Asuna everything is chill."

"I'd never use that word."

"She'll think you're being ironic."

"This is really starting to blow," Van said. "Blow hard."

"Guns, phone hacks, this cop car," Scott said. "Who the fuck are you people?"

"Our worst nightmare," Leah said.

They drove into the Queens Midtown Tunnel.

CHAPTER THIRTEEN

The block reminded Leah of cereal boxes in her cupboard at home. Thin rectangles, slightly different heights, except for that one on the end she'd turned to face out, because she didn't want to forget out about it. A special açai berry, quinoa, super combo that cost as much as a palatable cocktail. Eating it would make her look like the woman on the box and still, every morning, she couldn't bring herself to pour a bowl.

She'd dig into it now if she had it. Crap. When did she eat last? She couldn't stay up this late and not snack.

Dani's apartment building looked yellow in the cast of the street lights. Banana pudding yellow. It had four-pane windows, spaced like nutritional information. Thick sills. The kind that would have had window boxes back in the forties, when, she guessed, the place opened to tenants.

It posed a tactical challenge. The front and back doors could not be seen from any single vantage point. She needed a partner to cover both the front and the alley behind the apartments. If she were Dani, and Dani were as easily freaked as her friends, she'd dart out the back the second Scott called. Or the front. Either. She didn't know this chick.

She looked at Joshua. He sat casually, his right knee up against the passenger door, gloved hand resting on top, the backs of his fingers tapping the window, purple and black check shirt still pressed and fresh. His hair rolled slightly back and to the right. Dark, silky sheets and turndown service.

"All right," she squeezed out of her mouth, her rational brain fighting to keep the rest of her statement inside. And losing. "You watch the front. I'll position myself in the alley. You call me if you see her. I've never seen her, but I'm going to question any redheaded millennial that runs out into an alley at midnight. Got it?"

"It will be my pleasure," Joshua replied.

She took Scott's phone, got out and walked around to his side of the car. She opened the door and handed him the phone.

"She didn't answer the text," he said.

"People respond differently to a call at midnight," Leah replied. "Call her."

"And say what? Some people are looking for you?"

"Honesty is the best policy, don't you think?

Scott moved to take the phone. Leah didn't let go. He kept his eyes on Leah's. She could tell he felt conflicted. He no longer wanted to do what he had wanted to do. Not now that Leah wanted it, too. Which left him what? No choices. He pressed Dani's name on his phone.

Leah pressed the 'speaker' button on his phone. They all listened to it ring.

"Scott?" a young woman's voice came up from the phone.

"Yep," he answered.

"What's wrong?" She sounded concerned.

"Some people are looking for you. If you're not——"

Leah pressed the mute button.

"Scott?" Dani called out. "Scott, are you there?"

Leah shut the door. Scott slammed his hand on the window.

"If you're not what?" Dani continued. "Not what?"

Leah walked to the corner and turned.

"Shit, shit, shit, shit—" Dani ended the call.

Leah skipped up to a light run. She didn't know how fast this Dani girl could move. Young, an entertainer, she might be in great shape and pretty damn quick. Leah got to the entrance of the alley that ran behind the buildings. A thin chain link fence blocked her. It had a latch but no lock. She pushed and entered, trying to be quiet, happy for the first time that night she'd worn the official color of New York professionals. The black jacket and pants made her harder to see.

She dropped Scott's phone into her jacket pocket. It clicked against two shotgun shells. She drew out her own phone and pressed *Joshua Fawls.*

"Hey, Leah," he said. "How have you been?"

"Any sign of her yet?"

"Nothing. Nothing at all. This is the quietest spot in Brooklyn. Good thing I don't need a cab."

"Not when you've got me."

"You might have a future in the Gypsy cab business."

"Is that what your crystal ball tells you?"

"We don't actually use those." The color of Joshua's voice darkened a shade. Leah might not have even noticed if she weren't alone in a black and white alley, with nothing else engaging her besides his baritone lilt—on the cusp of musical, with all traces of an accent brushed out. *Sfumato*—soft smoke. No barriers, no boarders, no lines. In this case, no lines leading back to a place. No origin.

"We?" Leah repeated. "I was making a Gypsy cab joke. What are you talking about? Are you a Gypsy? I'm sorry, Roma?"

"I don't identify with any one group," Joshua said. "I'm psychic-fluid."

"I didn't realize you were psychic at all," Leah replied.

"That's because you're neurotypical. There's no shame it that."

"Well, thank you for—" The back door of Dani's apartment building creaked open. "—nothing." Leah raised her voice and started to slur. "I didn't call you because I wanted to get back together."

"Pardon me?" Joshua asked.

A young woman dumped out into the alley, both hands buried in a large, orange Miu Miu knockoff. Assumed knockoff. Maybe this girl spent a wad of her art thief money on a great bag.

"I don't want to get back together," Leah whined. "Why does it have to be like that?"

"Perhaps you're not as neurotypical as I thought," Joshua said.

The alley offered little light. Still, the woman couldn't have been thirty years old, hundred-twenty pounds, much over five-seven or anything but a natural redhead. She had the soft freckled skin of some-one who'd go with you to kill some English.

"You make things sooooo difficult," Leah doled out.

The woman brushed by her, not looking up. Plowing towards the gate.

"I take it Dani's made her entrance," Joshua said.

"You got that right!" Leah turned and bounded.

She reached the gate as the redhead did. Leah jammed her foot against the bottom of chain-link so the woman could not pull it open. The woman twisted, tucking her arms in as she realized how close Leah stood. Her face contorted.

"Hey, lady," she snapped. "Do you mind?"

"Are you Dani?" Leah slipped her phone into her pants pocket.

"Do I look like a Danny? Let me out."

"I think your name is Dani and I think you were at Lexington Park this morning."

"My name's Ella and you're making me late for my shift."

Leah took Scott's phone out of her jacket pocket.

"Where do you work?" Leah asked.

"Listen, you crazy-ass bitch. Move your fucking foot or we're going to have a problem."

Leah poked in Scott's password, then pressed the number last called on Scott's phone. "What kind of problem? Financial? Meta-physical? We already have a relationship issue."

A song came from the large handbag. Drums and whistling.

"Why don't you answer," Leah said. "And we can talk this out."

The Dani's face stretched, chin to eyebrows. If Leah had pulled out an axe, she didn't think the girl would look more horrified. Dani darted to the right, looking to shoot out of the corner. Leah blocked her, arms wide. They were pretty close to hugging now, Leah thought. Too close.

"Settle down," Leah said. "I'm here to ask questions. That's all."

"Let me go!"

"You're scared. I get that. I'm scared, too. For a little boy."

Finally, Dani met her eyes. Leah didn't smile. They weren't there yet.

"I think you were at Lexington Park this morning and you pinned a note on a little boy's jacket. You'd been hired to do that. Just pin a note. It's not even illegal, right? Just weird. But all these rich bastards are weird."

Leah stopped the phone from recording a voice message and slid it back into her jacket pocket. Dani said nothing, which disappointed Leah a bit.

"You didn't think you were doing anything wrong," she continued. "Not terribly wrong, anyway. After the whole scene—that's when you put things together. That's when you got scared. This wasn't some rich bastard's practical joke."

"I don't know how you got my name or found me, but—"

"You are a clever woman, Dani. You realized right away I couldn't identify you by your face. Calling yourself Ella. Smart. Don't stop being smart now. Who asked you to pin that note?"

The sides of Dani's face dropped, pulling the corners of her eyes along for the fall. It let Leah see the fullness of her dark irises, almost as black as her pupils.

"I don't know," Dani said.

"You don't know what?" Leah returned.

"I don't know who asked."

"How did they ask, then?"

"Email," Dani said. "I got an email."

"How did they pay you?"

"Cash in an envelope. They pushed it through my mail slot."

"How did they get your email address?"

"I don't know that, either."

"You didn't think about it?"

"There's lots of ways. I've got it all over the place. Every time I go for a part, a bunch of people get my email address. I make it pretty easy to get my address. I want people to have it."

Leah heard someone approaching on sidewalk, outside the gate. More than two people. Heavy but casual.

"That little boy was kidnapped, Dani," Leah whispered. "That was a ransom note you pinned. You have absolutely got to give me something here."

Dani's eyes welled. Leah had already decided not to believe any of the body-language Dani might telegraph. This type of girl could cry on cue.

"I don't know anything," she said with a tremble. Leah kind of believed that touch. The tremble came from fear.

"Hey," Joshua said as he approached the gate.

"Hey," Leah said back.

"Oh man." Dani's tremble got worse.

"It's alright," Scott called from a few steps back.

"Speak for yourself," Van added. "My nuts are still roasting here."

"You brought the whole gang." Leah bowed her head.

Joshua spread his arms. "You expect me to walk around this neighborhood alone?"

CHAPTER FOURTEEN

Dani's apartment would be awesome, Leah thought, were it a walk-in closet. She didn't begrudge her the smallness of it. She had to turn sideways to get into her first apartment in the city. The clothes, though— the room had a two steel pipes chained to the ceiling, staggered, and each packed with skirts, dresses, gowns, jackets and what she thought might be a mermaid tail. The contraption took up a good third of the three square feet Dani called home.

The couch had once been lovely. Hunter's green velvet. Mostly. The last of the three bottom cushions was midnight blue. She almost got away with it, as the clothing on the lower bar partially concealed that whole end of the sofa. The room had two chairs. Spindles of fake maple with soft, wheaty seats. They matched the two-tiered coffee table, covered in magazines, books and sheets of white, three-hole punched papers. Scripts, perhaps. Stacks and stacks of the things.

The room had two closed doors. Kitchen equipment made up the rest.

Scott and Van lobbed themselves over the coffee table and landed in the couch. Dani stood with her back to the racks of clothes.

"Where is the envelope?" Joshua asked Dani.

"The money?" Dani asked back.

"I could not care less about the money. I want the envelope it came in."

"Shussh." Dani patted the air down with both hands.

"It's not hush money," Joshua said.

Scott laughed.

"I don't want a call from my neighbor." Dani knelt down next to the coffee table and stuck her hands into a stack of papers. They were definitely scripts. Plays or screenplays, Leah didn't care enough to look. Clever hiding place, she decided. No one else would care enough to look in there.

Dani drew out a standard white envelope. She removed a slim stack of bills from inside and crumpled them tight before Leah could see the sizes or denominations. She handed the envelope up to Joshua.

"There's no return address, you know," she said.

He took it and moved into the kitchen area.

"No, really." Van woke up. "Who are you people?"

"You don't act like cops," Scott added.

"You don't act like you're not cops, either," Van said.

"They could be cops that are bad actors."

"Or bad actors playing cops."

"We're just bad," Leah said. "As in ass." She watched Joshua turn the envelope over in his hands. Gloved, he examined it as one might a newly discovered Spenser manuscript or letter from John to Abigail.

"Which one of these doors is the bathroom?" Joshua held the envelope up so the light from the ceiling fixture would pass through it.

"That one," Dani jutted her head in the direction of the door behind Leah.

Joshua disappeared inside.

"Who are you people?" Leah asked. "Was Joshua right? Are you an improv troupe that moonlights as art thieves?"

They bounced glances off each other, playing some silent version of the telephone game. The message may have been muddled when it got to her, but Leah understood the gist of it. These kids held a secret between them. Not the surprise party kind.

Leah started visiting art galleries at a young age. In the womb, according to family lore. Her mom and dad made galleries the focal point of each family vacation. Through the babbling course of her memory, Leah found, in paintings and sculptures, marble halls and hushed corridors, her personal version of skipping stones or molding sand castles.

In galleries, Leah could perform for her parents. Make them smile. Together. With those knowing looks similar to the ones these kids were making, only of the more pleasant, non-conspiratorial variety. Her parents liked to lead Leah to a painting and tell her nothing about it. They stood quietly while she absorbed details and then told them what she thought, as if she already had her master's degree, at age eight. She'd go on about colors, images, perceptions. They always got a kick out of it. So she always did it.

Always. She liked art without preconceived notions. She almost quit school on ten separate occasions because getting good grades, recommendations and acceptance turned out to be, so often, the reiteration of preconceived notions. Not conceiving new notions, the very reason she had passion for the subject in the first place.

Her current job utilized her gift of wonder more than her last job. Go figure. Leah realized early, at the FBI Academy, that the absorbing of details, with no preconceived notions, was not just a way of approaching art. It was the way to approach art crime as well.

Back to work, she said to herself. *Let's see more of this picture.*

"It's just," Leah started, "you don't seem like art thieves. You don't seem like you're *not* art thieves either. You know how that goes."

"Indeed we do." Van nodded.

"What are we doing here?" Dani asked.

"Joshua had to use the bathroom," Leah answered.

"With my envelope?"

"These two are not what they seem," Scott said.

"What do they seem?" Van cut in. "Really. It's creeping me out, man. I don't even know what they don't seem like."

Leah sat in one of the spindly chairs and looked at Dani. "Who hired you to steal the Modigliani's *Nude Sitting on a Divan*?"

"Who told you I did that?"

"The guy in the bathroom," Scott said.

"Fuck this shit." Dani's head panned the room. Looking for a way out. Of everything, Leah decided.

"It could be the same person who hired you this time," Leah said.

They did not exchange glances. The boys were confused. Leah wanted that to continue. They were more manageable the less they knew. She wasn't here to emit. She wanted to absorb. Still, she needed to get them talking.

"Listen," Leah said. "I don't care. I mean, not right now. I've got bigger fishheads to fry. I get how hard it is to make it in this city. To make it anywhere. Work, audition, work, audition—half your pay goes to rent, the rest to food. You're left with nothing else besides hope. Then someone comes along and offers you money to take something from an insanely wealthy guy, just so some other insanely wealthy guy can have it. It is a victimless crime. This other business, though. Dani—that's got victims. Innocent ones. So, please, who is this guy?"

"We don't know," Scott said.

"We really don't," Van added.

"Total cloak and dagger stuff."

"Remember that last meeting?" Van asked.

"In the church?" Dani joined in.

Van chuckled. "God almighty, what a production."

"A repurposed Anglican church on 37th," Scott explained. "We met the man running the show. He had these nutty stage lights on us so we couldn't see him. Like we're trying out for *A Chorus Line*, right? He talks to us through a sound system that auto tunes his voice. I swear to God, I thought maybe Daft Punk was rebooting *Punk'd*. Daft Punk'd."

Scott and Van chuckle hard, until Dani flaps her hands.

"Enough," she says. "This isn't helping."

"We can't help," Scott said. "We don't know the point."

"There was that whole *Wonder Woman the Musical* thing," Van said.

"That's not going to happen." Scott looked at Leah. "Is it Special Agent what's your name? Foxy McBossypants?"

"Sassy Pantellones," Van snickered.

"Whipyourass," Leah said. "Special Agent Whipyourass."

"Fuckity fuck." Dani stared.

The bathroom door opened and Joshua emerged. He carried the envelope in his right hand and both of his gloves in his left.

"We can go whenever you're ready." Joshua pulled on his left glove.

"You didn't flush," Scott said.

"Or wash your hands," Van said. "Gross, man."

Joshua moved his gaze from Scott to Van to Dani has he slid his right hand into the other glove. He looked across his shoulder at Leah and said, "I'm all done here."

CHAPTER FIFTEEN

Leah let Joshua sit up front again. She didn't have to. They had
no passengers for their ride out of Brooklyn. She just . . . she didn't know.
After one-in-the-morning on a work night, she didn't know. Except a little
boy had been taken from his home and she had, most certainly, mis-
handled every aspect of everything from the NYPD call at 9:00 PM until
now.

As the city flicked passed the lightly tinted windows and the too
cool air agitated from the black vents, she wanted to put the windows down
and smell the mofongo cooking and diesel fumes and bacteria breaking
down things people no longer wanted. Never lower the windows, she'd
been told by more seasoned field agents. They never told her the reason.
Safety? Distance? Mystique? She leaned heavily on that last one. The FBI
coveted its elite status. Leah—not so much. She joined for one reason.
Now she had found another, unwarranted and really, truly unwanted.

Wants. It's always about the wants.

"I have a number of questions, Mr. Fawls." Leah watched the
street. "Why don't you start talking and we'll see if any get answered?"

"My apartment's in the Village," he said.

"I know," Leah replied. "Your current address is the only thing in your file."

"I have an FBI file?"

"You do now. I started it. You are licensed to operate a non-commercial motor vehicle in the State of New York. And a motorcycle."

"They're cool."

"You have known for some time who stole the Modigliani."

"Yes." Joshua leaned back in his seat. "Since about two hours after it happened."

"For more than a year, then."

"Yes."

"You told no one."

"Why would I?"

"Because it's a crime?" Leah blurted. "Because it's actually the greatest heist in twenty-five years? Hell, because of the reward, if you weren't feeling too civil-minded."

"None of that is enough." Joshua shifted in his seat. Leah could feel him looking at her. She could feel the connection forming, like slender rose vines slinking across an invisible trellis. Tough, but supple. Sweet with a sprinkle of tiny, budding thorns.

"Enough." Leah had intended to make it a question. It didn't come out that way. "Not enough for what?" She fixed it.

"Enough to . . ." Joshua paused. Leah saw, through the corner of her eye, a slight huff. A glance upward. A minor change in Joshua's body she found major. He was not a sharer and he was about to share.

"You met those kids," he started. "They took a marker from one rich guy and gave it to another. A marker. A chip. One of those stones in Go. That's all these things are to these guys. Some of them, anyway. A way to get over on a rival. Or perceived rival. They usually don't dare compete where it matters. They keep their competitions high and meaningless. Until it gets nasty. If I had told anyone what I knew, Scott and his cohort would, at best, be in prison. Their lives ruined. At worst, they would be dead."

"Dead?" Leah said. "You believe that?"

"Is it any harder to believe than kidnapping a four-year-old boy?"

"You kept this secret to protect them?"

"Until tonight." Joshua shifted again, to face out the front windshield. He tugged on the gloves on his hands. "They don't get to skate on an innocent child."

Leah glanced at him. He sat staring straight ahead, city lights glistening in his eyes. She had dealt with con men before. Intimately. They were the center of her vocation. Her newfound passion, if she wanted to be honest with herself, which she didn't, because she didn't have time for that shit. She no longer trusted her gut. She'd stop doing that three years ago. Without her gut, she had to look at Joshua—with his big sleepy eyes, jaw tight to keep any more emotion locked and stowed—and decide if he was a nice, caring guy, or the slickest conman ever.

Slickest since Archibald Lee, anyway.

Archibald Lee had walked into The Wen near closing on a Friday. Hair black with enough silver to let you know this wasn't his first time doing anything. He wore it swept back. It looked like he moved while standing still. He had the kind of tan you get on the bow of a boat, a Glen plaid suit simultaneously old and new, and he finished the ensemble with a pink shirt and white ascot. The ascot got her. You couldn't pull off one of those if you weren't superbly confident. Which, by no coincidence, is the origin of the term conman. Short for confidence man. She knew this at the time and paid no attention, distracted as she was by his cheekbones and his large portfolio—the kind one uses to transport art—handcuffed to his wrist.

Gorgeous men and handcuffs. Did she have a type? Was it the worst, most embarrassing type imaginable?

Archibald Lee tilted his head. He raised his eyelids like stage curtains and smiled—long, deep, convincing.

Leah sauntered over. No. She walked like always. Never distract from the art, she'd been told, and never had she received a more useless piece of advice.

"You are quite fresh," Archie said in an accent.

"I apologize," she replied. "I didn't think so."

"I mean to say you are new here." An Alexander McQueen—Wimbledon-Claridge's accent.

"Month number three," Leah returned.

"My name's Archie," he had said. "You don't have to give me yours, but it certainly would make my day if you did."

As Leah remembered it, she introduced herself directly and welcomed him to the gallery.

"What interests you?" Leah asked, trying not to stare at the leather case bound to his wrist.

"At the moment," he replied. "You."

There was no one else in the gallery, but she didn't feel uneasy. The windows, the lights, the cameras—she always felt safe in the space, and this man did not put out signals to counter it.

"Capello," he repeated. "Italian, but you don't sound like . . . how should I put this . . . one of those distinctive New York Italians."

"You mean like bada-bing? Fugitaboutit?"

"Yes," Archie grinned.

"A professor found me and learned me to talk like a regular lady."

Archie laughed, tossing his head back. "Lord help me, she's as quick as she is beautiful. I'm smitten."

"And I'm a failure," Leah said. "You are supposed to be smitten with the art."

"Yes, well, you've made for a tough act to follow."

"What brings you here?"

"How did *you* end up here?"

Leah grinned herself. "I inquired, they made an offer and here I am. The Wen is a wonderful space."

"No, no, your journey," Archie said. "There are a thousand roads to Mecca. Which one did you take? Were you raised in an art colony? Were you born into it, your family home one of those mansions on the Cape that should just go ahead and admit to being a museum? Are you a scrappy girl from Hardscrabble USA, making a show of it in the big city?"

"Wouldn't you rather tell me what's in the portfolio?" Leah asked.

Archie looked left and right with just his eyes. He seemed to ponder her question, then lightened his face. "I am betting you are House of Grimaldi, a duchess, determined to prove yourself, even if it means—sigh—getting a job. You're going to show everyone that you don't need the monarchy to survive. I can see it the delicate taper of your eyes."

"I get that a lot," Leah said. "If I had a dime for every time someone said I looked like a duchess of . . . "

"Monaco," Archie filled in.

"Duchess of Monaco, I wouldn't need this job."

Archie smiled. Tiny lines spread from the far corners of his eyes. Soft, tan fireworks.

"Sadly, I do need this job," Leah continued. "So I'm going to do it. How can I help you?"

"You have been helping all along," Archie said. "Chatting with such an enchanting woman has been quite a help."

"I didn't do anything."

"I'm not sure you could." Archie made a slight rotation towards the door. "No offense."

"But I am offended," Leah said. "I don't think you've given me a chance to assist you."

"I am sorry." Archie bowed from the waist. "I should be going."

The only mix more dangerous than champagne and chocolate is a cocktail of secrets and charm. With intoxication, comes boldness. She asked, "What's in the case?"

Archie turned to her with a look that made her feel admired.

And that, Leah chided herself, in her government sedan, skimming through Brooklyn, *is why you're going to clear your head right now. You don't have enough time, resources, or inner goddess for this shit. This guy is another one. Another fine-looking, erudite, scam artist art maven with a smile that makes you gushy and you are the pillar of your own life and if your life gets gushy it tips sideways. Topples. Fawls.*

No more hustlers, Leah yelled in her head. *Get pro and stay that way.*

She took a breath and said to Joshua Fawls, "You have been fully, or tangentially, involved in four crimes. That I know of. That is what we call a pattern. I don't want to say a 'pattern of criminal behavior', but once can be bad luck, twice is a coincidence, and four times is a lifestyle choice."

"Four?" Joshua raised a white-cotton fist. "There's a Modigliani . . ." He popped his fingers up in succession. Counting. "The kidnapping, that business with the Cezanne two months ago. That's only three."

"I found you chained to a hotel bed," Leah said.

Joshua's fourth finger extended.

"Not to mention," Leah continued. "Stepan staged an art theft to get me to find you. We should really call it four and a half."

"I see your point," Joshua said.

"Yet you are never the criminal. You're always nearby. Around. You're not even an accessory to these crimes. More like a crime accessory."

"Like the perfect clutch."

"How?" Leah asked. "Just how?"

Joshua blew a lung full of air out his nostrils. They approached the entrance to the Queens Midtown Tunnel. He laughed with what little air he had, inhaled and said, "You will not like my answer to that quest-ion. You're not the type."

"And what type would that be?"

"You are a detective, of sorts. Logical."

"Are you going to give me more of that psychic crap? Like you did on the phone? What did you call me? Neurotypical?"

"This is not a conversation I want to have," Joshua said. "If you haven't noticed, we haven't had it yet, because I would rather discuss politics, religion or my sexuality than talk about how I acquire my special knowledge."

"You've never voted, haven't been to church since your tween-years and you like women. A lot. Feel free to fill in the gaps."

"Wow," Joshua said. "Are *you* psychic?"

"I'm a woman," Leah answered. "You've never been married, you're self-employed, with a healthy income, college-educated and have a strained relationship with your extended family."

"If you're not a telepath, how'd you get that last one?"

"You changed your name," Leah said. "It wasn't always Fawls. I could tell by the lack of material in your file. People don't do that if they have strong family connections."

"You're not entirely wrong." Joshua smirked. "You're not entirely right, either. But. Regardless . . . Alice, you are about to tumble down the rabbit's hole."

They zoomed into the tunnel.

Leah sighed. "Did you stall so you could use that line right now?"

"Do you blame me?"

CHAPTER SIXTEEN

"Are you familiar with the term psychometry?" Joshua asked.

Leah looked at him. In the striking white lights of the tunnel his five-o'clock shadow inched into a wee hour territory—into the I've-been-out-too-late time that this freakin' city cultivated like a crop.

"It comes from the Greek," Joshua continued. "From the words soul and measure."

Why did he have to use those pillow lips to form words? His voice had a fine Bourbon quality. The words, though. They were from the well.

"Personally," he kept talking. "I don't care for the word. It tries to define the activity, but instead it confines it. Reduces it. The effect it tries to describe is not easily reflected in words."

"Is that why this all sounds like so much bullshit?"

"Yes," Joshua replied. "No matter how you talk about, it sounds stupid. Psychometry has a nice, sciency ring to it. It's way better than saying I get vibes from an object. Or I can read an object. That takes us from pseudo-science to hippie to Victorian séance. After that, most people end with charlatan."

"Whoa," Leah said. "You weren't kidding before. You are going with psychic."

"Also not a great term," Joshua replied.

"You don't like to be pinned down by the language, huh. I see that a lot in my line of work."

"I imagine you do."

"From con men."

"Yes," Joshua sighed. "That is what most people think when the subject first comes up. I don't dissuade people from it much anymore. It's easier to have people think I'm a carnival act than spend countless hours convincing them I'm the real deal. It is rarely ever worth it. Kind of rarely. Tonight is presenting me with exception after exception to my various rules."

"I know exactly how you feel." Leah bulged her eyes. She didn't want to think about how many codes, procedures and maybe even laws she might have brushed over tonight. "Learn the rules like a pro, so you can break them like an artist," Pablo Picasso said. Except her art form was what again? Tangents?

She blinked hard and asked, "What exactly is your talent?"

"It's better if I show you."

"As promising as that might sound to some women, how 'bout you tell don't show?"

"No, really." Joshua twisted in his seat and leaned towards her. "What have you got that's personal? An object."

She could feel him looking her up and down. "Nothing," she said.

"No rings." Joshua leaned closer. "No necklace. No bracelet. You don't even wear a watch."

"Nothing." She drove down Park Avenue. She didn't know if this was the quickest way to his apartment. She didn't like doing math this late—or early.

"Nothing!" Joshua exclaimed. "But that's my trick. My thing. That's what I do when I need to impress someone. I take their silver cross and explain how it was given to them by their grandma for their First Communion; or how their ring was handed down through three generations of pompous misery; or a watch they bought in St. Croix on a whim on a cruise during a mistake with a guy who turned out to be fun only after your third Cuba Libre."

"I know how that feels," Leah said. "Anyway, I don't care. I want to know where you're getting your insider information."

"That is what I'm trying to tell you."

"That you are psychic."

"I read objects." Joshua clunked the left side of his head against the plastic mesh that rose up from the car's front seats. "Why don't you have any?"

"You tell me, Professor Spooky."

"Please, call me Joshua."

"Josh."

"Joshua," he said. "Josh is something you do in fun."

Leah turned her head and looked at him for as long as the street would allow. A bit longer, actually. She returned her attention to the cars and signs and lights a third of a second before rear-ending a box van, double-parked, no cone. She zipped around it. What street did he live on again? West 11th? What had she been about to say?

"You don't wear any accessories either," Leah said. "No jewelry, which is not uncommon. No watch, which is less so. Guys like you tend to have a TAG Heuer on their wrist."

"You never met a guy like me."

She put the car on West 11th and sped up a bit. The driving had gotten old. The conversation had gotten her nowhere. The drain of response chemicals in her body had left her thirsty and tired and sick of sitting on fake leather with cold air blowing across the knuckles of only one hand. They didn't match. She wanted her hands to be the same temperature. She wanted out of this stupid car and this stupid conversation and this stupid, stupid night.

Stepan Markov Jr., four years old, no more than forty pounds. Blond hair, blue eyes. Should be blue. Probably red from crying because he's never been away from his parents this long and this late.

"Where's your place?" Leah stared straight ahead.

"Up there on the right." Joshua motioned his gloved hand in the direction of skinny building with a closed storefront.

She couldn't be bothered to read any of the address numbers she might have been able to make out. It didn't matter. She saw a loading zone a couple yards down from where he pointed and nosed the car in. She got out of the car and stretched, arms straight, entwined and high over her head. She locked her knees and pumped up and down on the balls of her feet. The village smelled different than Brooklyn. More salty, less fried, but retaining that underlying scent of unguided fermentation.

As Joshua emerged from his side of the sedan, Leah walked around. He had a quizzical look on his face. He held his arms out, as if playing an invisible piano. White gloves flashing in the glow of the street lights. He didn't know what to do with his arms, Leah realized. Or his face.

He didn't have the right body language for a situation he didn't understand.

"I thought, you know . . . " he stammered. "You'd drop me off."

Leah crossed her arms and looked down the street. "Which one?"

"The hat place," Joshua crossed his own arms, and tossed his head back and to the right.

Blood red brick, with brain gray mortar. Squared off, in careful repair. A huge picture window took up the ground floor, framed in glossy black. Chic, Leah thought. The window had gold and red words, encircling a cartoon fedora. 'Hats Blocked Here' painted by Barnum and Bailey's guy on the off-season. Behind the glass hung a thick, drawn curtain. More gray. Next to the window stood a glossy black door. Its window had sign that said, "Sorry. Back in whenever."

Back in whenever seemed cute at first. It wasn't like Joshua actually ran a hat blocking business, because nobody did, because no-body wore hats, so nobody would be pissed off. Put another way, the whole thing was a lie. He didn't block hats, so what was he up to?

It pricked at her. The question.

She'd been at Cocoon Two for about a year when Micky Swanick came in. Caucasian, blond, and the size of a small turkey, he seemed to be powered by raw electricity. He had a set of canvases wrapped in the brown butcher paper. Most artists came calling with high quality prints—much easier to lug on the train. If the gallery wanted the work, they'd send someone for the originals. Micky insisted that only the originals did his work any justice. He took out the first one.

A white canvas. Leah didn't know what to say.

"It's called *White*," the artist said.

"I might have guessed."

"It's not blank," Micky said. "Look closely."

Leah took the piece, held it up and scrutinized it. Brush strokes, layers of oil paint—all white, all the same hue. She could only discern any work at all by the texture. She titled the canvas, using the ambient light to catch the rises and falls of the paint. She brought out an intricate cityscape, most likely New York, so pale and faint it took a good dollop of her imagination to define it.

"Huh," she let out.

"I paint using one paint."

"I see. Kind of."

"I've done other color studies, too," Micky continued.

"Huh," snuck out again.

Paintings people couldn't quite see. He put hours and hours into details the viewer could never make out.

Clever or pointless, she had asked herself.

She didn't know and she wanted to know and she couldn't figure him out. Coy, cutting edge, complete waste of time? What was he up to?

Leah went and found the gallery's owner, Magdalena Brown, and convinced her to take on Micky Swanick. She couldn't let him go. Not yet. It would be like putting an Agatha Christie book down halfway through.

You can't let him go until you learn what he's up to. Leah stood looking at the sign painted on the glass. "You don't block hats."

"Which is not to say I'm opposed to it," Joshua returned. "You are inviting yourself up, then?"

Leah took a step forward. "You examined Stepan's note, told him you knew nothing and took off, running your own cowboy investigation. I got to be your sidekick, because I can park anywhere in the city."

"As far as super powers go," Joshua said. "It's among the more useful."

"Now you've examined Dani's envelope, and said nothing, and I get the feeling you're trying to ditch me. You don't need my super parking abilities, so you don't need me." Leah walked past Joshua, towards his front door. "The reverse is not true. You are wrapped up in this business like a freakin' mummy and I'm not letting you out of my sight until I get it all unraveled."

She stopped at the door. New brass knobs and lock. She corrected herself. A sophisticated German locking system she'd only ever seen on museums and high-end galleries.

"Invite me up," Leah said. She put an edge to her voice, so it didn't sound so suggestive.

Joshua slid between Leah and the door. Joshua reached into the mail slot and pulled out a small, glowing green keypad. He typed six numbers with gloved fingers and slid the pad back into the slot. Leah heard multiple bolts retract.

"Special Agent Capello." Joshua pushed open the very black door. "Would you like to come up for a night cap?"

"As long as it's a stiff one," she replied.

Damn, she shouted in her head. Why did she speak? She should never talk this late. People didn't have productive conversation after midnight.

And she was simmering herself down to rock bottom real fast.

CHAPTER SEVENTEEN

Joshua Fawls' storefront-brownstone deserved its museum-grade security system. The street door opened into a small foyer. Wrought-iron stairs—amber puddle lights helping one find their footing—led upwards; a doorway on the left led to a what had, once upon a time, been a toy store or antique shop or modern art gallery, probably all at different times, each leaving a bit of itself behind in the changeover. The bare lighting would enable navigation, not exploration, so Leah couldn't be sure of everything she thought she saw through the door's glass. Still . . . A rack of six Roman amphorae, looking as old as the earth. A pithos, almost as tall as her, with intricate carvings from lip to base. A motorcycle, World War II era, with a sidecar. Clamped to a studio easel she glanced by what could have been an original Francis Bacon—one of his figure studies, the body a swirl of naked tension. She couldn't remember the name. A cabinet that looked fourteenth-century Spanish. A space helmet, on a treasure chest, next to a footlocker. The walls had more. More of everything. Her eyes couldn't find a place to rest. She looked up and saw a woven basket big enough for four.

"That is a special piece," Joshua said. "Off a hot air balloon."

Leah closed her eyes—she noticed then that the air did not reek of musk and rot like so many collections. She aimed herself at the stairs, opened her eye and started upward. She heard Joshua following behind her.

The top of the stairs ended at a landing, with a frosted door. Joshua scooted by Leah, careful not to touch her. Very careful. He couldn't have had a quarter inch to spare, she decided. And then decided not to be insulted. He had a thing. Not even casual brushes, even after being held at gunpoint together. Even after seeing him mostly naked. Kind of. Fine. This wasn't the end of a date.

As the door opened, the second floor lights began to glow. Recessed and dim. Just enough to let one find a bar or bedroom. She half-expected the Barry White to start playing softly. The room had the expanse of the shop below it, with one brick pillar near the center keeping the next floor up. A cone-shaped, orange enamel fireplace in the corner. Cute. A faux fur area rug. An Eames lounge chair next to a green tweed sofa. Built-in shelves and cabinets and curios surrounded it all. The room did not have the haphazard clutter of the first floor. This was neat, livable, comfy, if a bit masculine.

"What can I get you?" Joshua asked as he entered.

"Bourbon," Leah answered. She continued into the room. She wanted to see what this infuriatingly peculiar man hung on the main wall of his apartment.

Blank. She kept walking. A nail protruded from the center of the far wall, near the fireplace. What a shame. Joshua crossed behind her. She turned to look back out the second floor windows. He had light shades for privacy, but the glimmer of the Village still got through. She heard him clink glasses and walk some more. Looking over her shoulder, she could see his kitchen.

Fudge. Thin strips of teak, seamless concrete counters, more exposed brick, and lights suspended from marine chain that could have come off the *HMS Beagle*. Holy crap, she wanted to cook something just to be in there.

He clunked some ice into two rocks glasses and walked back into the living section. She turned to watch him this time. He had a bar on the wall to the left of the windows. Curved like a tongue depressor on the left end, broken off five-feet later, on the right. She guessed oak, slowly scorched by eighteen million cigarettes. The shelves below, housing an amazing array of liquor, were obviously recent additions. The mirror behind gave her reflection depth as only lead glass and real silver could. The bar, though. How flat and plain and worn to that juncture between intriguing and the curb.

Joshua turned and caught her staring at the unfinished end of the top. "I know it's rough." He had two glasses. "It's from the Cedar Tavern, though. Can't very well change a piece of history."

The Cedar Tavern, Leah repeated in her head. The Cedar Tavern. She couldn't remember where she'd heard that before.

"Resnick and de Kooning used to drink there. Jack Kerouac supposedly got banned from the place for relieving himself in a sink."

"Yes," Leah mumbled as vague memory surfaced. "Jackson Pollock used to hang with those guys."

"Him too." Joshua nodded. "They had to lob off this piece when the place moved. It's closed, now. But I got a piece."

He handed her a glass of brown liquid. He no longer wore his gloves. His hands looked fine. Great. Not that she was a 'hand' person. She didn't know if she'd ever paid attention to a man's hands before. At least, as objects. You always had to watch what a man's hands were doing. Girl 101.

Leah took a sip of her bourbon. Full, sweat, a little smoky. She liked the cool burn of it. And the familiarity. She'd had bourbon like this before and it had nothing to do with gloves or have balloon baskets or de Kooning's favorite bar.

"What are you doing here?" Joshua sipped his drink.

"I won't know until I say it," Leah replied.

"Fair enough." Joshua crossed over to the couch and flopped down. "Make yourself comfortable."

Leah made her way around to the other side and sat partially facing him. She noticed the coffee table now, littered with objects that fit no pattern she immediately understood. A gold cup, a marble obelisk, a pen and inkwell, a gray rock on a wooden pedestal. She didn't set her drink down.

"You can relax," Joshua said. "Give yourself permission. There is nothing more you can do tonight."

"I don't think that's true."

"That's because of all your government 'round peg, round hole' training. Trust me on this. We are in polyhedron world now. Whatever procedure you think you should be proceeding with is, well, I was going to say wasted, but I think it's worse than that. You need some rest. You will be better after some rest. We both will be. Tomorrow we can try again."

"I know," Leah said. "I know. I can't help thinking there's more. Another lead, another—"

"Not right now, there's not." Joshua lowered his head. "Yes, there are more people to talk to. And yes, they are all asleep."

Leah brought her nice, normal bourbon to her lips. "You convinced Stepan Markov you can read objects."

"I did."

"You need a suicidal level of confidence to attempt a trick like that. I mean, if he thinks he's being made the fool, it's not going to end well for you."

"I would still be hanging somewhere, begging to die."

"Yet here you are." Leah drank.

"There is no place I'd rather be." He saluted her with his glass and joined her.

"A couple of years ago I met a man from the U.S. Border Patrol," Leah started. "He was known as the human lie detector. He didn't like the nickname because he's better than polygraphs. They are about seventy-percent accurate. This man was close to one-hundred. Like a mind reader. He didn't even know how he did it so well. Years of watching and listening and even smelling people trying to get past him. He could have performed in Vegas as a genie, he was that good. Pay attention, he said. There's no magic. So, let me ask you. This thing you do with objects—reading them. Is it séance or science?"

"I wish I knew," Joshua said. "I've spent most of my life wondering. Doing my own testing. There is actually some research on the phenomenon. References to it go back thousands of years. The turn of the last century paid it some attention. Modern science has mostly dis-counted psychometry, though. Tossed it into the paranormal bin, with all the other unaccountable phenomena."

"Science has a method to its madness." Leah smiled.

Joshua smiled back. "That method likes things that are repeat-able and measurable."

"So you're not like Sherlock Holmes. You don't examine an envelope and say, it's sixty-pound linen from a specialty shop in Brixton, with a trace of Channel No. 5 . . . so it must have been Miss Scarlet, in the study, with a candlestick."

Joshua chuckled. He stretched and leaned back deeper into the crux of the sofa. "The first time we met. At that hotel. Stepan had asked me to stop by and authenticate that supposed Renoir you lured him to."

"We thought it was real," Leah said.

"And stolen."

"And he bought stolen art."

"I touched it," Joshua said.

"I remember," Leah agreed.

"I could see this shaggy, thickly bearded John Lennon type pouring himself into the paint. I could feel his anger. He had more talent that the great Pierre-Auguste Renoir and yet this knock-off would bring in a hundred times more cash than anything he ever sold on the streets of San Francisco, circa 1960. He wasn't Renoir. He hated Renoir for having the luck of being born a century sooner. The hatred and envy came through with every stroke and dab. The impression that he left—forgive the pun—"

"I can't."

"The impression had power. The painting captured this forger's energy. His anguish. His soul."

"Really."

"Truly."

"Except it can't be verified." Leah curled the left side of her mouth.

"I didn't catch a name."

"How convenient."

"I didn't catch a name *this* time," Joshua said. "Sometimes I do. A person's name is only part of their identity and not always the part they're putting into their work. This forger spent so much time thinking about Renoir, his own persona became lost in the painting."

"You are a convincing witness," Leah said. "If only you had evidence to back you up."

"Such is my curse."

"I'm sleepy," Leah said.

"I'll show you the bedroom."

Leah let her smile saunter across her face. "The couch will be fine."

"There are more than enough beds in this place," Joshua returned. "Guest rooms."

"No, really, the couch is fine."

"I have some silk jammies I think you will find quite tasteful."

"I kind of wanted to sleep near the door," Leah said. "That was the point of coming up here."

"Download a motion alarm to your phone," Joshua said. "Set it against the door and if I try to leave, you will know."

"There's an app for that?"

"You've obviously never been stalked." Joshua stood. "I'll lay out your pajamas while you set your trap."

Joshua went in to the next room and Leah got out her phone. She searched for an app and sure enough—there was a program that would sound the ringer if her phone was moved. She downloaded it, set her phone against the front door and activated the alarm. If he wanted to go out the fire escape, screw him.

Poor choice of words. She would not be doing that. Nope. She would sleep in this gorgeous, weird-ass, near-perfect stranger's bed. Nothing more.

CHAPTER EIGHTEEN

The jammies were exquisite. Blue and white stripped silk so soft Leah decided they were never coming off. She could easily wear them under all her clothes from now on. Who would know? She could be busting criminals in these fantastic pajamas and everyone would be better off for it. She'd be happy, do a better job, put more bad guys in jail. All good.

7:13 AM.

Not good. She had to get out of this bed, walk out into the strange apartment, with her hair a mess, no makeup, smelling like a bar rag—what the Hell had she been thinking last night? Hey girl, why don't you have the freakin' worst one-night-stand imaginable? No sex with the cute boy, just the awkward second part, where you stumble around hoping his eyes are still too blurry to see the real you. On a Thursday morning. When you're supposed to get to work protecting the nation from people like the one you went home with, more or less. Maybe.

She needed her phone. Leah swung out of bed, a task made easier by the marginal height of the frame. It stood only a few inches up from the floor on what appeared to be a single slab of birch. The sandy color worked nicely with the ash-gray sheets and comforter. Joshua had matching birch dressers on either side of the bed. Low, and uncluttered. Open birch cubes severed as night stands on either side of the bed. Pendant lamps hung down to meet them. Leather shades. Nothing else but a round-faced clock.

7:14 AM. Crap.

No clues. No family photos, books, magazines, Go Michigan pennant, mounted fish, golf clubs, or amber bottles of antibiotics. *So you might as well get moving*, Leah told herself.

She pushed open the door to the scent of coffee. She shook out her hair and padded out into the living room. She followed the smell to the kitchen. Joshua stood, staring into an iPad, holding a mug that matched the concrete of the island.

"Good morning," he said. "I hope you like French roast."

"Anything in the general coffee family would be great."

"Did you sleep alright?" He set the device down and moved to the far counter, where the coffee machine sat. Bright chrome.

"Surprisingly well." Leah planted her elbows on the island and her head on her fists.

"I don't have any cream or creamer," he said. "Not big on the dairy. I could run out to—"

"Black," she said. "When you drink as much of the stuff as I do, you learn to keep it simple."

"I can do simple." Joshua poured her a coffee and turned, smiling. He, of course, looked Sunday-morning cozy. The tussled hair, the extra beard, the plain white T-shirt and sweat pants. Bastard. She bet his breath smelled minty. He stepped back to the island and handed her the mug.

"Thanks." She held it close with both hands. Soothing warmth. Natural. Normal. Really, nicely normal.

"I snuck out last night," he said. "Through my back door. Tracked down a few more leads I had. Everything is fine now."

"I followed you," Leah returned. "And learned all of your secrets."

Joshua laughed without making a sound.

"I'm sorry about the phone thing," Leah said. "It seemed clever at two in the morning."

"It's OK. You don't know me."

They sipped their coffees. Leah soaked up the pause. The quiet. She knew it would not be lasting. She had about an hour to get her brain up and running, ready to perform all kinds of calculations for which she lacked the significant data.

More data. That's what she needed. She had, in her short career, only worked a handful of cases. Art crimes had a tendency to cover years, decades or even centuries. Clues were a rarity. She'd never actually seen one. Progress came from looking, listening, imagining, and turning page after page of catalogues, ledgers or briefs. It would be drudgery, were it not for the ... Eh ... nope. It was drudgery. She just didn't mind it sometimes. Like now.

"Who hired that improv troupe to steal the Modigliani?" Leah asked through the steam coming off her mug.

"I don't know," Joshua replied.

"You figured out those goofballs did the heist, but not the mastermind?"

"Nothing came through. Regardless of what you think about my talent, it really is how I access this special information. Oscar Pierce had me over to his place the day after the *Nude* was stolen. He's not a believer like Stepan. He thinks I know about forgeries and thieves because I know a lot of forgers and thieves. He thought I might have insight. I didn't. I did get the chance to look around, and I use the word 'look' metaphorically. The police missed one of the catering uniforms the thieves left behind."

Joshua sipped his coffee. Leah waited. She didn't have a clue—they were that rare—where the story might lead. But, as she just re-minded herself, she needed more data. This counted. Kind of.

Leah couldn't wait all morning. "You touched the jacket without your gloves on?"

"I did something I rarely do," Joshua said. "I stripped down to the waist and put the jacket on. Full skin contact all the way around me. I enveloped myself in the memories."

"The memories?"

"In the jacket. Look, I don't want to sound like a flake. I'm not one of those card readers who charges you twenty-five bucks to tell you your grandma misses you. Even if you paid me, I wouldn't tell you anything, but you asked, and, well, the alternative is worse. I don't want you thinking I'm a criminal."

"So you're going with wizard."

"I'm going with the truth," Joshua said. "Isn't that your grand pursuit? To get to the truth of things? Do FBI agents take an oath or vows or pledge or something?"

"You're thinking of a sorority," Leah said. "The FBI is nothing like that. And I mean nothing."

Joshua grinned. Leah took a big slurp of coffee. She needed more in her system.

"I'm not a wizard," Joshua said. "At least, not when it comes to object reading."

"Oh," Leah said. "You have other talents?"

He almost winked. She could see it, the slightest twitch of the muscles around his left eye. He stopped it, though.

"I put on this caterer's jacket," he continued. "I go all in and I get, what I call, the retrospective. An experience left behind by the last person to wear this jacket. I feel the nervousness, the jitters, the con-centration and the excitement. It radiates from the jacket. I realize these are not the emanations of a hired waiter. The last man who wore this thing had way more intensity than any waiter I've ever seen at any cocktail party. The person who wore this jacket experienced some of the strongest emotions of his entire life. Which is how it works."

"How your reading works," Leah offered.

"Exactly." Joshua's face brightened. "The stronger the emotions pumped into the object, the stronger the retrospective. It's like etching in stone. The deeper the cuts—the more energy the artist put into his hammer and chisel—the easier the etching is to see, feel, understand. And the longer it lasts."

Leah couldn't keep her head from tilting to the left. She didn't want it to tilt, nor did she want it to be this early in the morning, or the conversation to be this weird, or half of this whole situation.

The other half wasn't half bad.

"Skepticism is healthy." Joshua tilted his head to match Leah's. "Don't dig your Louboutin's in, though."

"Louboutin," Leah repeated. "I wish. Even if I could, I wouldn't. Do you have any idea what this job does to shoes?"

"No," Joshua said. "I've got the opposite problem. If I don't show up in looking like a Fifth Avenue mannequin, people won't think I'm successful enough to trust."

"Trust is everything."

"It's something." Joshua smirked. "It's up there with patience and devotion, sure, but it's not everything. Love, special Agent Capello. Love is the thing."

His look, through his eyes, into hers and down her entire nervous system carried a charge. Electrical. And comforting. Both, at the same time. She told herself to get out of that apartment now *and* get another cup of coffee, curl up in that Eames chair and see if he got the *Times*. Both, at the same time.

"Ok ok ok ok ok." She shook her head, as if it were an old Etch A Sketch and she could clear it and start again. "You saw Dani when you wore the waiter's jacket."

"The wearer was quite concerned for her safety."

"But not the person orchestrating the whole thing."

"Nothing even close."

"So that path of the investigation has dried up," Leah said. "You got to Dani but Dani can't get us to the kidnappers."

"I'm afraid so," Joshua said.

"Which means we back up and start down a new path. The note Dani pinned to little Stepan's coat told big Stepan to stay home tonight. That could have two meanings. Stay home, because you will be contacted about the next stage in this crime. Or stay home as in don't go where you planned to go."

"You're leaning towards the latter."

"You said he wanted you to be available."

"That is all he said."

"Other than reading the occasional kidnapping note," Leah said, "What does Stepan use you for?"

"Authenticating art." Joshua set his mug down. "We are friends. Good friends, I might even say. I've been to the house for vodka and borscht. Two of his houses, actually. But not all of them."

"You think there's a deal taking place tonight?"

Joshua nodded.

"And someone involved doesn't want Stepan Markov to be there."

Joshua tapped his nose.

"Does that mean 'on the nose'?"

"I can't do 'on point'," Joshua said. "Never studied ballet."

CHAPTER NINETEEN

Once again, Leah Capello maneuvered her black sedan through the streets of Greenwich Village, this time pointed at her own apartment. Leah put her fingers across her lips, pre-shushing her passenger. Joshua put his head back, closed his eyes and let mouth settle.

Perfect, she thought. She needed time to think. She did not find deep thought to be helped along by Joshua Fawls. Or the streets of New York on a Thursday morning. The two combined would have been catastrophic.

The day had plenty of spring brilliance. The kind of day that got people out and moving with more vigor than usual. The city never rested, but it did slow some in the colder months. It picked up around now. With results she considered mixed. No more bulky coats. Great. More orange cones, yellow trucks with diggers and racks of iron and glass, concrete barriers angled out to pinch traffic and force pedestrians into new patterns—not the ones they'd been repeating every day for the last four months. Not so great.

While Joshua rested or meditated or communed with her car, she tried to remember what she'd actually planned to do today, what she had planned back when she thought she had the ability to actually plan. What cases demanded attention. What meetings she had to attend, what forms she had to file, what she could put off, avoid, forget or abandon all together. If her memory served her, she could clear the day. She had confidence in the organizational portion of her memory—a skill she took from college to her gallery life and into her current position. Knowing when to do what had always been a critical skill. Right now, she felt sure this case-that-wasn't-a-case warranted her full attention. Everything else would slide.

She didn't know if her supervising officer Dean would see it that way, but shit. If she couldn't work him, she had no business in this business to begin with.

Leah had a place in an old building in the lower East Side. The address was great. Reasonably close to everything and not caving in. The apartment itself had its challenges. It had been re-carved from space created nearly a century ago, previously intended for domestic servants. Now intended for servants of the more general kind. Like her. A public servant.

She found a section large enough for her car, nosed it in and told Joshua they had arrived. He looked up, grinned and got out. They went in, took the elevator to the ninth floor and she dug for the keys in the inside left, zippered pocket.

"You don't carry a purse," Joshua said.

"The jacket is my purse." She inserted the key into her door's lock and paused. What kind of disaster might she have left behind? She ran out last night when the NYPD called. Was the place a freakin' pigsty? Did she put her laundry away or were various species of undergarments strewn all over her living room like a grenade went off on the ninth floor of Saks?

Too late now. She turned they key.

Leah's apartment had very little light. The living room had but one window and it hung so close to a similar window in the next building she didn't know why they bothered with two panes of glass. She had the blinds cinched most of the time. She walked in and turned to see Joshua's expression. She did not have people over often. When she did, she liked to see their initial reactions. No one could 100-percent hide their feelings.

"Mmmmm," Joshua said. "Pie."

"I call it home." Leah walked into her wedge of an apartment. The shape of the building had created triangular spaces at one end. Real estate profits created the opportunity to actually use those slices of pie-space for human habitation.

"I love it," Joshua breezed by her, into the center of the room. "The boundaries force you to think outside them. No couch cleaving the space, no television as a focal point. This is literally off center."

No one had ever passed her test before. Leah stood, gazing into his grin.

"Great use of color," he continued. "Nice and bright. Floral patterns. It livens up the room."

"Thank you." She took off her jacket. "I'm going to shower and change and you don't have to sit in here."

"You said you didn't want to lose track of me."

"I am . . . reassessing our situation."

Joshua turned to face her. He clasped his white-gloved hands in front of him. She started to think they actually went with his royal blue shirt and jeans. "I'm going to make a few calls and see if I can ferret out what kind of deal might be happening tonight. You go freshen up. I'll be fine."

"There's . . ." she started. "I don't know what there is. Yogurt. Grapes. Leftovers from Dan Choi's I didn't get to . . ."

"I'm fine. Really."

She huffed. Her shoulders dropped. She had no guide for this moment. No standard operating procedure for the man-crime mush she felt herself standing in. She wanted to be a host and she wanted to get to work and she really, really wanted to shower. Was that protocol?

Protocol. Time to have that word shot into her skull.

She closed her bedroom door, took off her jacket, took out her phone and called Dean directly, on his cell. She didn't know much about his morning routine, but he would not normally be at the office for another hour. She hated calling people at weird times. People's hearts jump at calls at weird times. Especially special agents.

"Leah?" he answered. Mild crowd noise, no echo.

"Did I catch you at a bad time?"

"Getting coffee. What's up?"

"I won't be in today," Leah said.

"Feeling alright?"

"I won't lie to you, either. I'm cultivating a civilian asset."

"What?"

"Civilian asset," she repeated. "Cultivating."

"You don't know how to do that."

"Are you kidding me? I *was* that."

"That doesn't mean you're an intelligence expert," Dean said.

"Kind of," Leah returned. "If you think about it. I was on the civilian side, now I'm badged. I've got more experience than most."

"There are careful protocols."

"I watched them exercised by the best."

A soft gargle of background noise. A woman called a name, another hollered a response. A church of heavenly brew. Leah let him steep in the complement. He might know she was playing him. He might not care.

"Who is it?" he asked.

"I'll catch you up later."

"How about now?"

"That is a very reasonable question," Leah said. "This is where I have to say 'trust me'."

"This cultivating is so time dependent we can't meet up and make sure you've got support?"

"I find it as hard to believe as you do."

More crowd noise. Another shout. Leah heard Dean chirp 'here' with the phone pulled, at her guess, an arm's length from his mouth.

"You should've called in sick."

"See," Leah said. "That's how you know you can trust me. I'm so honest I couldn't even spin a white lie."

"You make that sound like a good thing," Dean returned. "Honesty is not always a virtue. Not when you're working an asset."

"I've got a lot of brushes in my bin, Dean. I know when to use which."

"You know shit, Leah. You check in by ten or I'll have you picked up."

"Awesome. That sounded very nearly like a vote of confidence."

"That's how long it will take me to get to the office, track you down and dispatch a team. You'll be calling to talk me out of it."

"Yeah," Leah said. "OK, then. See you tomorrow."

She pressed the 'end call' button with one thumb on top of the other.

Leah showered, checked on Joshua—who claimed to be fine—put on some makeup and picked out fresh clothing. This day could bring anything, which made getting dressed a bitch. She needed her jacket again. The same one she wore last night. She didn't feel like switching all her stuff to a new one. She chose pants again. Light gray. Dressy but versatile. Yet another white blouse and she was back in the living room.

Joshua lay stretched out on the yellow comfy chair, feet on the ottoman, like he lived here. He held his phone up in one, gloved hand and tapped it with the other. Ungloved. He flopped in her direction when he heard her approach.

"Very nice," he said.

"That I'm clean?"

"That you look very nice."

"What did you learn?" She crossed to the middle of her living room. Joshua could return his head to a more normal position and address her.

"Nothing," he said. "I don't know what's going on tonight."

"When you told that story about Oscar Pierce and Modigliani, you said a rival had stolen the painting. It made me think you knew who did it."

"I got a feeling," Joshua said. "I had some facts and sensed a story that fit with those facts. What I have though, what I do frequently have, is pronouns instead of proper ones. Do you know what I mean?"

"At this very moment." Leah turned to the wall on her right. A print dominated the center. A Jeremy Mann painting of the city at night. A small credenza stood beneath it. Candles, a lacquered box and a couple of books. Leah pulled an old, yellow hardcover out. She straight-ened up and handed it to Joshua. He sat up, dropped his phone to his lap and reached to take it with his gloved hand.

"The other one," Leah said.

Joshua looked her in the eyes and brought down his hand. "Are you sure?"

"It's just a book I happened to have."

"You don't wear jewelry."

"I don't want any identifying items when I'm out in the field."

"You don't have many trinkets in your apartment."

"I've moved twice in the last four years," Leah said. "I travel light."

"I think you did before you got here."

"I'm not a 'stuff' kind of person."

"Which makes this all the more important," Joshua said, arms still at his sides.

Leah gently thrust the book towards him. Joshua raised his naked hand and took it. He set in on his right thigh and looked at it for a moment. The painting on the cover was of a teenage girl, a bobbysoxer. The cover itself was worn, but decent. *The Secret of the Old Clock*. Joshua pressed his right hand to the cover. He bowed his head, as if me might take an oath of pulp fiction office.

Joshua picked up his head. Leah saw an extra glistening in his eyes. Not tears, but perhaps the start of them. No. She wouldn't be matching those. Nope. She clenched her jaw. Joshua raised the book. She took it quickly and returned to the shelf. She didn't have to look at him if she took lots of extra care putting the novel back in place.

"You read it in some kind of dorm room," Joshua said. "But you weren't in college. You were about the same person you are now. Just about. You dropped a tear into an early page. Someone dear to you gave you that book. You started it the night you heard that she passed. She wouldn't see you graduate. Oh, if only she could have——"

"Got it," Leah snapped. "You are clever."

"I'm sorry."

"We're cool." Leah crossed her arms and stared down at Joshua, sitting on the edge of her chair. "Do you remember where Oscar Pierce lives?"

"I do," Joshua answered. "The typical midtown high and hidden palace."

"Let's visit."

"You know it doesn't work that way, right? Men like Oscar Pierce don't do drop-ins."

"You are going to lecture me on the impossible? Mmmm, probably not. Ever."

CHAPTER TWENTY

Back in the black sedan. Leah had driven more in the last twelve hours than the last twelve months combined. When she did get out in the field, she rode with someone else most of the time, mostly boys. The boys always liked to drive. She had no problem with that. She wished she could let this boy cart her around for a change, but that wouldn't work for several reasons, the first being she didn't have a bead on him. She should have ranked *he wasn't with the Bureau* first. In reality, her problem with Joshua had little to with his credentials. Or everything to do with it, de-pending on your point of view.

Credentials, as in credibility.

"What's the trick?" She asked as they drove up Park Avenue.

"I don't do tricks," Joshua said. "Do I look like a prostitute?"

"Actually—"

"Don't."

"You could probably do fairly well with a certain clientele."

Joshua held up his gloved hands and pulsed them like he was in a Bob Fosse show.

"Oh," Leah said. "That's right. No touching. That would limit your prospect pool."

"It's not polite to refer to people as objects," Joshua said. "But we're made of matter. Rocks, roads, Rothkos, Mark Rothko himself. It's all the same marble. It looks different in the Bellagio than it does after Michelangelo has spent some time with it. Marble is marble, though. Marble is also you, me and the David."

"So you can read people like you read objects?" Leah asked.

"No," Joshua answered. "Inert objects are like photographs. People are like movies. 3-D. In surround sound. It is not pleasant or welcomed or anything I want any part of."

"That's why there's no touching."

Joshua looked at her. She sensed it. Part peripheral vision, part soundscape, part feeling you get when you think someone's staring at you. In her experience, someone pausing this long had an internal 'plus' and 'minus' list they had to check before speaking. It usually occurred after a tough question. Not a confirmation, like she just offered.

"Sure," he finally said.

"Except for your friend last night," Leah said.

"Yeah," Joshua said. "Except for her."

Leah dared a quick glance at Joshua. No devilish leer, no dreamy eyes all glossed over with the memories of a long and lovely tryst. He looked almost sad. She had to look away. The street demanded it.

"I didn't mean to insult you before," Leah said. "About the trick."

"I take no offense." Joshua faced front. "It's not an easy thing to convey. Most of the time I don't even try. It's like getting someone to love a painting using a text message, you know? You can't do it. You've got to see the thing. Sometimes not even a photograph is enough."

"The first painting I ever loved was *Boy Leading a Horse*."

"Picasso."

"Yes," Leah said. "Part of the Paley exhibit. When it traveled, I got to see the painting in person. The dominance, the mystery, the mastery of what was there and the brilliance of what was missing—I understood all of art in that moment. And I can't tell you how or why."

"Thank you for sharing that."

"Um, yes," Leah tried not to stumble. "I should thank you. I don't get to share too often."

"What a shame," Joshua said. "You seem like the type."

I wasn't sharing, Leah said in her head. She only shared enough to get more. Alright. Not exactly. She hadn't dropped to that temperature yet. Right?

Right. She needed a moment to think. A moment better than this one. Go, stop, go, stop. Midtown, mid-morning traffic. It had no tempo, no beat. People didn't drive in this city because driving interfered with human brain patterns. A person couldn't think with so much stimulation and no way to resolve it. Half-mixed-sideways messages shot at you from any angle and at any time.

Stay with it, girl, she chided herself. You can walk and chew gum. Even if the gum is ginger-saffron-lavender punch.

"How well do you know Oscar Pierce?" Leah asked.

"About as well as I know anyone," he replied.

"What's it like—all this distance between you and the rest of the world? Is it carefree? Is it a little lonely? Or is it confusing? Do you always feel like you came in too late on the conversation?"

"Whoa." Joshua rotated, putting his left knee up on the seat. "I am sorry about the book. I was reluctant to touch it, if you remember."

"I'm over it." Leah looked for a hole in the stream of cars and trucks and things that go. She wanted to move this trip along. But no. She couldn't break from the herd.

"If you say so." Joshua kept looking at her. Why? Why the freak did the freak keep looking at her all the time?

"It's answers like that last one that bug me," Leah said. "You said 'As well as you know anyone.' What's that supposed to mean? You know everybody to the same depth? Really? Everyone?"

"I've talked to him twice," Joshua said. "I've been in the same room with him a half-dozen times. A couple of private auctions. Very private auctions. One party, a gala—fund raising for finger paints or something. One morning after the theft of Modigliani."

"That's an answer." Leah glanced at him. His eyes changed like the seasons, if the seasons cycled every twenty minutes. Perky to hot to wistful to sad in seven blocks.

"He made his money in real estate," Joshua continued. "He had to. He would have been fired by anyone who thought they could be his boss. He buys land to own it. He builds towers and golf courses and strip malls for the same reason a dog urinates in its yard. Marking his territory. Mine, mine, mine. He buys art because he can't create. He can only acquire. That does not make him unusual in the art world. His competitiveness does. The acquisition is the art for him. The taking. Which is, I guess, how you make an enemy angry enough to steal and hide a masterpiece."

"Huh," Leah blurted. "You know everyone that well?"

"Yes," Joshua returned. "Everyone."

"You'd make a decent FBI agent."

"Or 'art and antiquities consultant'. Not that there's much of difference."

"No one in the Bureau can afford a three-story in the Village."

"There is that," Joshua said.

Leah saw a 'no parking zone' at the start of the next block. She deposited the car and got out. Joshua did the same, put his elbow on the roof and took a leisurely lean.

"What makes you think we can just pop in on this billionaire?"

"I don't." Leah took out her phone. "Doesn't stop me from trying, though."

She checked the time. 9:07. She groaned, thumbed through her contacts and pressed the one she needed.

After three rings, she heard the deep, sandy, "Good God, darling. The hour?" In only five words, the woman's eastern European accent managed to roll out like fog.

"I'm so sorry, Magdalena."

"If something is so terrible you need to phone at this hour, you should be phoning the hospital, I think."

"Sometimes what we need most is not a doctor," Leah responded.

"You don't come around, darling. How is that?"

"It's awful," Leah said. "I'm terrible at my new life. I'm still working things out."

"I know something about new lives," Magdalena said through the phone. "It should not stamp out your old one. No?"

"No," Leah said. "Listen, I'm on a case and I think you can help."

"Me helping you in your new life? You flatter me."

"Can you text me Oscar Pierce's personal number?"

"Oscar Pierce, the pile of shit? . . . Shit. Am I on the speaker?"

"No, Magdalena. Just you and me."

"You need to talk to him now about FBI business?"

"And you are better at connecting people with people than the FBI."

"Alright, darling," Magdalena said. "If you promise to come see us soon. Tuesday. At a proper hour."

"I promise."

Leah ended the call and looked at Joshua, who looked at her, small curl in his curly lips.

"I should bring you," Leah said. "Mags would like you."

"Magdalena from Cocoon Two?"

"You know her?"

"Through stories," Joshua said. "I like that gallery."

"I'm surprised you know it," Leah said. "It doesn't deal in the Renoirs and Cezannes of the world."

"My world is more broad than that."

Leah's phone vibrated in her hand. She glanced down and saw the contact Magdalena sent her. She took a deep breath and pressed the number on the screen. After a few rings, a woman's voice answered with a simple "Hello."

"I need to speak with Mr. Pierce," Leah said with flat confidence.

"May I ask what this is concerning?" Young. Poised. An ever-so-slight accent she couldn't place.

"His engagement this evening."

"Is there a message I can convey?"

"Yes," Leah said. "If it's still important to him that he attend, he should call this number."

Leah ended the call.

"You sure know how to sweet talk 'em," Joshua said.

"Sometimes sweet," Leah said. "Sometimes savory, sometimes a kick in the mouth."

"What made you think Oscar was going to this mystery event tonight?"

"Players got to play," Leah returned. "If whatever's going on is big enough to attract Stepan, and he called you—"

Her phone buzzed in her hand. No ring tone.

"Hello," she answered.

"I have grown very tired of this cloak and dagger routine," came a strained, older male voice.

"I apologize," Leah softened her voice. "I don't like to do things this way either. Why don't you tell the doorman to let me up and we discuss arrangements in person?"

Pause. Leah let it linger.

"Who is this?" the man asked.

"Someone who's going to keep you out of trouble," she answered. "At least for one night."

Another pause. Leah could hear them man breathe.

"Fine," he finally said. "Take off all your clothes in the elevator. I won't receive you otherwise."

"Fine."

She poked the 'end' button and looked at Joshua.

"What did he say?" he asked.

"To strip and come up."

"Even my gloves?"

"He wasn't specific."

CHAPTER TWENTY ONE

The elevator door parted, revealing a gun barrel, a black automatic pistol Leah couldn't identify from the angle. A woman held the weapon properly. Dark complexion, black hair with curls you can't get with an iron. Severe features, taught stance, in the type of slacks and blouse Leah herself might have picked out. Dressy, with allowance for movement. Leah would have profiled this chick as law enforcement if she hadn't led with the lead.

"Clasp your hands behind your heads," the woman said. No accent. This had not been the woman Leah spoke with on the phone.

"If I could reach—" Leah started.

"Clasp your hands behind your heads!" the woman ended.

Leah did as she asked. "Whatever."

She saw Joshua do the same thing. He said, "This is getting old."

"Tell me about it," Leah agreed.

"Exit the elevator," the woman commanded.

"We were going to do that anyway," Leah said.

"Why are you antagonizing her?" Joshua asked.

"She's being rude." Leah stepped out of the elevator.

"I wasn't talking to you," Joshua returned.

Leah chuckled a little, inside.

"Face the wall," the woman with the gun said with a bit more force. Leah smiled. The poor dear needed to be taken seriously.

"And spread your legs, Joshua," Leah said. "She's going to want us off balance and easier to search."

"Quiet," the woman said.

Leah and Joshua faced the wall, arms up like wings, legs spread too wide for comfort.

"That's perfect," Leah said to Joshua. "Have you done this before?"

"Once or twice." He winked.

"I said quiet," the woman snapped.

"Quiet is not what you need," Leah said with syrup. "You need information."

"I'll take the information I need." The woman positioned herself behind Joshua.

"Start with my right breast pocket," Leah said. "That's the ID I wanted to show you."

The woman peeled Leah's jacket open, pressed it to her back with the butt of the pistol and pulled out Leah's black leather wallet. Leah could hear her open it, then feel the pressure of the pistol fall away. She glanced over her shoulder and caught Joshua doing the same. The woman with the gun held Leah's open wallet up to a print on the wall. A cityscape, multi-media, which include, Leah decided, an active camera lens.

"Why didn't you identify yourself?" the woman asked.

"Why didn't you?" Leah asked back.

"I'm not the intruder."

"I had an invitation." Leah turned. The woman had relaxed some, but not completely.

"The invitation was for you and naked." She pointed her side-arm at the floor and held Leah's wallet out and open, her FBI credentials flapping.

"Sorry for the misunderstanding." She snatched her wallet back. "I thought it was business casual with a 'plus one.'"

The door on the left of the entrance hall clicked.

"He locked you in here with us," Joshua said. "Nice boss."

"Go on." The woman motioned towards the door.

Joshua opened it and stepped aside to let Leah enter first. The gold and pearlescent room had chairs and low tables and curios in the corner and several tons of drapery. Leah didn't know what to label the space. "Living room" did not fit. It seemed more the opposite. A mausoleum?

Two gold trimmed, pearl satin settees formed a corridor down the middle of the room. A man stepped into center and planted himself at the end. Bald but for a ring of white hair running from ear to ear. He wore dark jeans and a sport shirt, one of those Italian kinds Leah saw on wealthy tourists. This one was robin egg blue with gold speckles on one shoulder and looked absolutely ridiculous on anyone over thirty, which this guy had more than doubled.

"See," he said as they approached. "This is why I hate paying taxes. It goes to people like you."

"Good morning, Mr. Pierce," Leah said.

"I don't know if you remember me . . ." Joshua held out his hand. Pierce looked down at the glove and reeled back, exaggerating his astonishment.

"You're Markov's boy!" Pierce said. "Of course I remember you." He smiled and patted his hands downward. "Sit please, and explain to me why I'm not calling my lawyers. I mean, that is why you didn't announce yourself, am I right, Agent Capello? You want to try to deny my rights under the law?"

"I'm not going to lie to you." Leah declined the invitation to sit. "Not now, and not before on the phone. I really do want to keep you out of trouble tonight."

"Are you wearing a wire?" Pierce scanned Leah like his eyes used x-rays.

"No," Leah returned. "And neither is he and none of us are getting naked to prove it."

"You took that off the table pretty quickly," Pierce said.

"Who's running the show tonight?" Leah asked.

Pierce looked at Joshua, grinning. "She goes right for it, huh?"

"If tall, dark and efficient is your type . . ." Joshua sat. Leah watched him wink at the woman behind her.

Pierce returned his attention to Leah. His smile dropped. "Why don't you know who's doing the show? I thought you came here to tell me something. Keep me out of trouble? Not that I believe that. The two of you making a house call makes no sense to me, which means I am missing something. I am ignorant and I don't enjoy ignorance, so why don't we start there? Please, Agent Capello. Illuminate me. Educate me."

Leah turned at the waist to face the woman behind her. "You can relax. I'm here to be received, not to take."

The woman's upper lip wriggled. Nothing more.

Leah sat across from Joshua, and stretched her arm back over the settee. "The man who took your Modigliani is going to the private auction tonight."

"You know who took my *Nude?*" Pierce's know-it-all smirk vanished.

"It's not as simple as that," Leah said. "I know he's going to be there."

"How? How does that work?"

"I need a list of people attending."

"I don't have that!"

"Who does?" Leah asked.

Pierce scowled. "This is ridiculous. You are in the public employ, young lady. If you have information regarding the theft of my painting, I demand you share it with me now."

"I don't have a name, Mr. Pierce. That's why I want the list."

"The auction tonight is so speak-easy, I don't even know who's putting it on."

"She does," Joshua tilted his head at the woman with the gun, standing back by the door.

"Vita?" Pierce looked down the valley of loveseats. Leah followed his line of sight.

Vita's lips parted a little, just enough to get caught.

"Vita," Pierce repeated. "Did you look into this event?"

"We were not going to let you go in blind, sir," she said.

"And what did you find?" Pierce held out his hands, palms up, and flapped his fingers. "Come on. I don't care what they hear."

Vita licked her lips, then said, "Tonight you are attending a private auction, for which there is no written or electronic trace. Word-of-mouth only, with extreme discretion. There will be one item available to those in the room and no one else. No long-distance bidding will be allowed. The event is being held by Neal Pozner."

"Pozner." Pierce looked down and to the left. He ran his tongue behind his bottom lip. "Huh."

"You know him, sir?" Vita asked.

"Nice guy," Pierce said.

"Bit of a wanna-be," Joshua added.

Leah said, "It's a start."

CHAPTER TWENTY TWO

Leah and Joshua sat down in the café. She'd never eaten there before, didn't catch the name on the window, and cared only about the temperature of the incoming coffee. The faint smell of steamed milk hung in a space littered with plastic-skinned booths and Formica tables. The menu had been laminated. You didn't do that if you planned on making too many changes. The place catered not to the residents of the building they had just left, but to the people who manned the doors, repaired the elevators, picked up the laundry, walked the dogs, carted water, groceries, children, or those tubes messengers always had strapped to their backs, as if everyone in Midtown needed blueprints in the next fifteen minutes.

"So you've—" Joshua started.

Leah held up one index finger then returned her hand to her phone. She needed both hands to text quickly. This would be a much better way of reaching Dean at the office. He hated texting, which would limit his questions back to her. She asked him for information on Neal Pozner and left it at that.

"Sorry," Leah said as she waited for a reply.

"It's not like we're on a date," Joshua said. "Not at all, as I would've taken you some place much nicer. Sarabeth's, two blocks over."

"Then it would be more like a date." Leah kept her head pointed down into her phone. Dean had texted the letter 'o'. She couldn't decide if that meant he sent the message before hitting 'k', or if he didn't know how to find the emoji with the open dumfounded mouth.

"We're on a case," Joshua said.

"I'm on a case," Leah said. "I don't know what you're doing."

"If I'm not on a case, and I'm not on a date, I guess I'm having a late breakfast in New York's most underwhelming diner."

"Are you one of those super healthy eaters?" Leah asked, still staring into her phone. "Chia seed omelets and buckwheat smoothies?"

"God no," Joshua answered. "What I want is for every calorie I consume to be good. Not good for you, necessarily, although that can be part of it. I want a meal to have some thought behind it. I want someone to select the ingredients, blend them together and plate the result from a plan."

"Like a work of art," Leah said.

"Yes," Joshua nodded. "Not a blob, mixed with salt, heated, and flipped into the vicinity of a starch."

"Do you want to hear the specials?" the waitress asked.

Joshua and Leah looked up.

"Two eggs over easy," Leah said. "With wheat toast."

Joshua said, "The same."

The waitress gave him a sly, knowing look and sauntered away.

"Eggs and toast can be amazing," Leah said. "Done on a seasoned griddle, by a cook who understands the right moment to slide them off— those few seconds when the yoke is turning from runny to hard, when it's viscous, like paint. When it will cling to your toast points like golden ochre on a brush."

Joshua stared at her, somewhere between bemused and befuddled, she thought.

"You know Neal Pozner?" Leah asked.

"About as well as I—"

"Don't."

"Know—"

"Say it."

"Anyone," Joshua finished. "He's a New Yorker by birth. Grew up in the weeds of the art world. His grandparents had a little shop for years, which he lived at as a kid. Neal's parents sold it when they were offered an ungodly amount for the building. Neal watched the wrecking ball smash it and then watched one of those tall, skinny light roast buildings go up."

"What?" Leah said. "You two grow up on the same stoop?"

"He cozied up to me at Basel Hong Kong in March. Tried to ply me with liquor and tales of his childhood. Hoped we'd have a moment."

"Another disappointed customer?"

Joshua did jazz hands above the table. Leah returned her face to her phone, willing it to receive something. Which it did. An email from Dean, with an attachment. She opened it and read less prosaic details about Neal Pozner: Five-ten, thirty-seven years old, no warrants, one traffic ticket two years ago issued in the Bronx, an address in Brooklyn, a current phone number.

Leah punched it into her phone, grumbling that Dean didn't know how to send it the right way, so she could make a single poke as opposed to seven. After a handful of rings, Neal's voice asked her to leave a message.

"Sorry to bother you, Mr. Pozner. This is Special Agent Leah Capello with the Federal Bureau of Investigation, and I have a question or two about your event tonight. A call back would be greatly appreciated."

She ended the call and set her phone on the table, screen up.

"What was Neal doing at Basel?" Leah asked

"He didn't say directly," Joshua answered. "Which is not unusual. Most people go there to be there. Those with a purpose will be the last ones to tell you about it. Have you ever been to one?"

Leah shook her head. "I was still learning the trade here in New York when I heard my true calling."

"Bureau business hasn't taken you to one yet?"

"You'd be amazed how much desk-time I put in."

"You're making up for it now."

"I wouldn't mind a little—"

Leah's phone quivered on the slick, sky blue Formica. She picked it up, read the screen and waited through another ring.

Then she answered in a chipper voice, "This is Leah."

"Neal Pozner," came the voice. Bright and business-light, high pitched, but not pinched.

She said, "Thank you so much for returning my call."

"Anything for the FBI," Neal replied. "How can I help?"

"I need a list of the people you invited tonight."

Joshua's eyebrows bounced when he heard that.

"Wow," Neal said. "And here I just said I wanted to help."

"Yes, you did," Leah said.

"Nothing would make me happier than to provide assistance to the FBI, and please, if there is anything else I can do name it, because as far as my list goes, I can't hand it over."

"Sure you can."

"This is a very sensitive event, tonight. I'm not quite sure how you found out about it, to be honest."

"I need the list, like, well, right now," Leah kept her voice friendly. "That sounds pushy. I know. It's just, well, this is soooo time de-pendent."

"I don't imagine you have a court order or anything?"

"Now why would I need that?" Leah asked. "That request would imply criminal activity and I don't think your auction constitutes the premeditation of crime, does it? I wish it did." Leah added a chuckle. "That would make things easier. The reason I need the list has a relation-ship to your auction that is tangential at best."

"I don't see—"

"No." Leah stopped him. "You don't."

The waitress arrived with the breakfast plates. Leah watched Joshua smile and whisper 'thank you.'

"My clients value their privacy," Neal said.

"Then I will keep this private," Leah said back. "No one else is going to know I have this list. Like I said, I'm investigating a matter that has nothing to do with tonight, other than someone on the list is involved. That's pretty muddy. I'm sorry. I prefer to speak directly, but you know how it goes. God, of course you do. The art world mandates a bit of circumlocution now and then, doesn't it? I can't say much, but I can say this: I'm looking for a big wig. A mover and shaker. So I called the biggest player in the city right now. You. I'm betting your list has the largest whales in town. I'd looooove to see who you've got on there."

"I'm not sure."

"I'm sure your list is the best. But. Well. Mr. Pozner, you've been very kind. I won't take up any more of your time. And I do appreciate the time you've spent with me. I'm sure I'll see you around."

Leah dabbed her phone, set it down and exhaled.

"That was our lead," Joshua said.

"Our one and only," Leah replied.

CHAPTER TWENTY THREE

Leah and Joshua ate their eggs. At nearly ten AM, the café had less bustle than when they walked in. Leah would not categorize it as quiet—no place in the city ever fit in that category. Here, she could think, though. She could think about that little boy from the photos on the wall of Markovs' apartment. A beaming blond, bursting with energy—his father looking so far from a billionaire, she would have had a much different opinion of him had she seen the photos first.

Joshua slouched in his seat so he could slide his phone out of his front pants pocket. Leah dipped her toast into her egg yoke. She had next to no appetite, but the eggs were perfect and she knew she needed the protein.

"Lidiya," Joshua answered. "No, No. It's fine."

Leah didn't think twice about listening.

Joshua smiled at whatever he'd heard. "I can do better than that. We're having breakfast right now."

Leah rolled her eyes.

Joshua moved the phone away from his face. "She'd like to talk to you."

"Tell her to meet me at the park," Leah said.

Joshua repeated her request, said they would be there in about thirty minutes, and ended the call.

"You want to return to the scene of the crime?" Joshua asked.

"Two birds and all that," she answered. "If this were a proper investigation, that's the first thing we would've done."

"We're not very proper, are we?"

"Not in the least."

"I thought we'd be further along by now," Joshua said.

"Really?" Leah replied. "How's that?"

"I have a talent for learning things," Joshua said. "It frustrates me that now, when it really matters, that talent hasn't served me better."

"Then make it." Leah scooped up the rest of her eggs.

Joshua sat up. His gaze went up and over her right shoulder.

Leah took out her phone and called Dean. "Checking in," she said when he answered.

"You got the Pozner stuff?" he asked.

"Yep."

"Is he the civilian asset you're pursuing?"

"No."

"Good," Dean said. "Not a high value prospect."

"You know him?"

"No. That's why I can say that."

"Oh," Leah replied. "You know all the players?"

"No," Dean said. "That's why we got you."

"He's a stepping stone."

"You know what you're doing?"

"That's why you got me."

He ended the call or she did—it wasn't clear.

Joshua set down his fork and picked up his phone. "Can I have Neal's number?" He slipped his right hand into his left, under the phone it held.

"Think you'll have better luck?" Leah tapped her phone and sent him the contact info.

"Not better. Different." Joshua slid his right hand out of its glove. "I'm sure if you had had a face-to-face with Neal, you would have gotten what you needed."

"I'm not as persuasive over the phone?"

"You were fighting with one hand tied behind your back."

"Or handcuffed to a bed post," Leah said.

Joshua chuckled as his phone pulsed. He poked it a couple of times. "Thanks." He held it up to his ear.

Smooth, Leah thought. So fluid and kind of elegant. His mannerisms were practiced. He knew how to wear gloves so well he made it seem natural. Almost fashionable.

"Neal," Joshua said. "It's Joshua Fawls. I've got a Francis Bacon to unload and I think you might be just the right person. Ring me back when you have the chance. Cheers."

"Cheers?" Leah said as Joshua brought his phone down.

"Do I question your techniques?"

"Are you really looking to sell that Bacon I saw at your place?"

"We're all just caretakers, aren't we?" Joshua partly asked, partly said. "The great art of the world should be tended to. Cared for. Not hoarded or—worse—speculated with, like pork belly futures. Owning a piece can certainly be part of that tending to, caring for, process. When it changes, though, when you start to think someone else's art is yours, it's probably time to let it go."

Leah blinked twice. Then she asked, "Is it real?"

Joshua opened his mouth to answer but his phone quivered. He smiled, tapped and brought the thing back up to his ear.

"Thanks for calling back," he answered. And paused.

"Yes," he continued. "A mixed media piece—gouache, pastel, pen and ink, on paper. The provenance is, of course, absolutely unquestionable. I got it from one of Bacon's special friends. I'd love to show it to you. In fact, I'd like to give it to you. For the list."

Leah locked eyes with Joshua. She pressed her lips tight so her jaw wouldn't dent to Formica. He didn't smirk or wink.

"Your guests tonight . . . I don't joke about such things . . . Listen, I'll text you my address. Be there at noon. It's that simple . . . Great talking to you again. See you soon."

Leah smacked both palms to the table. "You've got to be freakin' kidding me."

Joshua spread his arms. "What?"

"That painting is worth a fortune."

"Eh. A small fortune." He drooped his hands and turned his head. "This moment is probably the reason I had it to begin with."

"That . . . " Leah couldn't decided how to finish the sentence. Was there any logic in there?

"You were right about the eggs." Joshua looked down at his plate. "They were little wonders."

CHAPTER TWENTY FOUR

Leah and Joshua did not speak as they returned to the car. Everything she thought to toss at him, she knew would be batted down. So she didn't bother. This guy wanted to trade a million dollar painting for a guest list. She couldn't stop him, even if she wanted to, which she probably didn't, as someone on that list had kidnapped Stepan Markov Jr. Still . . .

"There are other ways to see who's coming tonight," she said as they neared the black sedan.

"Not timely ones," Joshua returned.

"I don't know your per capita, but shit. An original Bacon? Would Markov do that for you?"

"I'm not doing it for him."

Leah heard a change in his voice. A breath of extra air escaping, rather than sailing out with a sail full of confidence. She thought he might follow it up, but he closed his mouth.

"When you called Pozner," Leah said, "you didn't re-identify yourself. I thought you'd say 'Joshua, from Art Basel Hong Kong'. Give him a reminder. You know?"

"He didn't need one." Joshua settled into his seat.

"So it would seem." Leah started the car. "You can make an impression. I'll give you that. How did you run into him?"

"Ah," Joshua said. "Did I meet him like I met you? No. There was no FBI sting or attempt on my life."

"With a cheese knife." Leah pulled out into traffic.

"A very sharp cheese knife. There was Pecorino Romano on that plate."

"You don't know that."

"It takes a capable knife to—"

"Neal. Basel. You," Leah said. "I need to know the circumstances."

"I didn't realize my social life was that important."

"Really?" Leah waved her hands like crazy. "Your social life got me conked in the head with a room service tray. Your social life is important if it's going to get me conked on the head again with a room service tray. Your business life is even more important."

"Sadly," Joshua said, "that's even more private."

"We're a little past that, don't you think?"

"Why does this matter?" Joshua asked.

"I don't know," she said despite herself. She didn't feel like sharing; she wanted *him* to do the sharing. She had learned, though, that sometimes the best way to get a ball rolling is to give it a push. She needed to share, and that was not her specialty. "I'm not a trial lawyer," she let out. "I don't ask questions if I know the answers. I'm an investigator. I ask all kinds of things. I never know what's going to be important.

"So I'm like two months into my first assignment, here in Manhattan, when I get a hit on one of the deep, dark sites I'm watching. Some idiot is trying to fence an Inca idol. I cross check it with a database of missing antiquities and sure enough, it had been reported missing three weeks prior. We bring this idiot in and talk to him. He says he found it. In Central Park. He actually has the audacity to ask if there's a reward."

"It's always good to have a backup plan," Joshua said.

"I like to put everything I've got into my first plan," Leah said. "Backups weaken your commitment."

"Or that."

"We can't really prove this guy stole the idol," Leah continued. "Selling stolen antiquities is illegal all by itself, but the penalties aren't the same. And we know we're missing something. I decided to re-interview the staff at the brownstone from which this treasure was taken. Gardener, handyman and maid. The maid's cute, right? About the same age as the idol thief. I start talking to her about all kinds of stuff. Where she lived, what she liked to do, where she went to lunch and she mentions that park across the street. She tells me she brings a sandwich and watches the kids on the swings and the dandle."

"The what?" Joshua sneered.

"I know, right?" Leah urged the car through the tiling of other cars and carts and the carriages that rolled around in this part of town. "The dandle. I looked it up and it's another word for see-saw."

"You mean teeter-totter?"

"That's exactly what I mean. No one calls them dandles. No one outside of Rhode Island, anyway. So I check and this maid is from Narragansett. And I remember that this thief is also an out-of-towner. I check his file and what do you think I found?"

"Your idol thief also came from Rhode Island," Joshua replied.

"Narragansett!" Leah said. "A town of fifteen-thousand people. What are the odds?"

"They knew each other?"

"They dated in high school."

"Aww," Joshua stretched out. "Were they robbing from the rich because they were so poor? Was Maid expecting a little Thief junior because if they could just get a leg up, a head start, they could make a nice home for the child?"

"He had a meth problem and she didn't like going to clubs in her uniform." Leah pulled over at the edge of the park. Another 'No Parking' zone. Another little triumph. She spun on her seat, cocking up her leg. "You never know what's going to be important."

Joshua let his head fall to the side. He exhaled. He tapped his fingers on the knee he bent up against the passenger door.

"I was a bit misleading before," Joshua started. "When I said there was no sting and no cheese knife. The rest of the scene you'd find familiar. Neal and I met in one of the private conference rooms they set up at those art fairs. Rooms for the actual dealing. Stepan asked me to authenticate a painting. A Kandinsky. Quite lovely. Quite fake. Neal was there on behalf of another buyer. After my examination, Stepan declined to bid. Neal seemed ready to buy, but our change of heart changed his heart. We all left the seller with that sad smile you see at wakes. Or wed-dings, when you don't think things should have gone the way they've gone."

"And he bought you a drink," Leah said.

"He tracked me down a little later," Joshua returned.

"What did you say?"

"I don't know. It was Hong Kong. Probably 'Gin Fizz, please.'"

"No," Leah said. "About you and your talent and Stepan Markov."

"He asked how I knew the Kandinsky was a fake. I gave him the usual stew of technique and palate and maybe I threw in something about urgency. I love using that word. Everyone thinks they are supposed to know what it means so they don't argue with you."

"You didn't mention your touchy-feely gift?"

Joshua turned in his seat. His eyes found hers and she felt a push or a pull or a plunge, she couldn't fully tell, what with her reason momentarily impaired.

And we're back, she yelped at herself. Crimes to solve and all.

"Special Agent Capello," Joshua said. "I don't share that with anyone."

But you did, she said in her head. *With me.* She let that roll about in her head for a moment.

CHAPTER TWENTY FIVE

Lidiya Markov sat in the park. Coral jeans, knit print top and turquoise chiffon scarf. A short one, knotted on the right. Holy crap, what a look. Did you have to be a billionaire to pull off that kind of flash? A billionaire *and* European? Leah figured if she showed up at the office with a chiffon scarf, the boys would ask her what she did last night and where did she find a guy who still gave hickies?

Three kids played in the park. Leah identified two nannies, and one bald man in a black suit on the edge, in the corner, so he could see both entrances. He had some years on him, maybe as much as fifty. He stood from practice. There are techniques you learn if you're going to be standing for hours—relaxed shoulders, loose hands, even weight distribution, the proper alignment of your back, so that that all the vertebrae are stacked and steady and not straining against a curve. Gravity hates a slouch. This man was no slouch. He'd learned how to manage his two-hundred pounds.

Due to his sunglasses, Leah couldn't tell exactly when he sized her up, but she threw him a smile when she'd finished with him.

"Is that Boris?" Leah asked as she sat down next to Lidiya.

"Yes it is," Lidiya responded.

"It is nice of you to keep him on."

Lidiya looked at Boris, expressionless. "He'll never let something like this happen again."

Joshua nodded to Lidiya and stood to the side. He nodded once to Boris. Boris continued to watch the breadth of the playground using the slightest movements required.

Leah asked, "What can I do for you, Mrs. Markov?"

"You don't have any children," Lidiya answered.

"No, I don't."

"You would not have asked that question if you had children."

"Does your husband know you're here?"

Lidiya's head snapped around. Her scarf fluttered. Her face stayed even. Leah thought, *The lady's got skills*.

"He is doing what you should be doing," Lidiya said.

"I'm not so sure of that," Leah returned. "I can tell by his play in the gallery that he's not a man that sits around. Especially when he's told to sit. I have a feeling that whatever he's doing today is even more desperate than the stuff he pulled yesterday. Stuff he shouldn't be doing. Stuff I wouldn't do and don't want to know about."

"I want my son back," she said.

"I know."

"Whatever it takes." Lidiya fixed her eyes on Leah's. "Anything."

"I'd like to talk to Boris," Leah said in a soft voice. "Can you call him over here?"

Lidiya pushed her head a bit in Leah's direction. A dare? An affront? Leah didn't understand the body language. She guessed the woman wanted to say more and thought better of it. She waved her bodyguard over with a single flick of her three tallest fingers.

Boris moved towards them. Moved, Leah thought. Not really a walk. He made an advance, like an army.

"This is an FBI agent," Lidiya said. "She has questions."

Boris nodded.

Leah looked up at the man. "Can you take off your sunglasses?"

He hesitated for moment, looking at her through two legless beetles pressed to his face. He slipped them off. Leah could see why he'd been reluctant. The layers of wrinkling fat pushing against the red rings of his eyes reminded her more of a couple of a Shar-Pei than the scorpion he'd been going for.

"I need to see your hands." Leah pointed at his glasses, then moved her finger to point at Joshua. Boris handed over the sunglasses. Joshua took them and backed up out of her sight.

Leah put her hands out flat. Boris mimicked her. She bent closer to the creases and callouses. His skin was tough on the palm and first joint of the index finger—he practiced with his firearm. He had hard islands of yellow at the base of his pink fingers. He lifted weights. Diligent.

"How many people were on the team?" Leah looked up into the man's face.

"I don't know." He had a sub woofer for a voice box.

"Sure you do," Leah urged. "How many would it take?"

"I don't . . . Four plus a driver. That is the lowest amount."

"Coffee guy, dog girl, look out with a note, and a snatcher."

"I put another in the street to make sure the car is clear. Maybe not. More crew, more risks."

"Yeah," Leah sat back. "I'm sure cost is not a factor here. No ransom. People talking, though. Especially hired hands. That's the trouble."

Joshua handed Boris the sunglasses.

"You are fine with my man?" Lidiya asked.

"It seems you are," Leah responded. "That says something."

"I have money. Money that Stepan does not know."

"We're fine," Joshua interjected. "And Stepan doesn't need to know about that, either."

"No, Joshua. I . . ." Lidiya lifted her head to address him. "My little Styopa. He is the world."

"I know."

"The world." Lidiya reached out to him. Her arms hung, in the air, like tree limbs, leafless in the winter. Joshua stood still and Lidiya's arms slowly fell back to her empty lap.

Leah stood. "Mrs. Markov, I am going to do everything in my power to get your son back."

Lidiya set her gaze out over the playground. "I think power may be why he is gone."

CHAPTER TWENTY SIX

Leah turned the steering wheel, glancing at her watch as it rolled passed her line of sight. 11:10. Plenty of time to get back to the Village without using the lights or sirens, plenty of time to trade Joshua's painting for a list of tonight's potential kidnappers, not even close to enough time to track down each name on the list, pay them a visit and somehow, someway, and by some kind of miracle get one to admit to one serious crime. An inescapably serious crime. These guests would all be wealthy enough for a solid defense but nobody walks on a kidnapping charge. Not for a four-year-old boy.

Presuming the perpetrator made it to trial. Leah had read Stepan Markov's file.

"Styopa?" Leah asked.

"The diminutive of Stepan," Joshua answered.

They came to a stop at a red light. Leah turned to him. "What did you see?"

"You wanted me to put those glasses on?" Joshua turned to her.

"That's why I had Boris hand them to you."

Joshua snickered as he relaxed into the seat.

And he put them on, she thought. Without a word. They worked together, like a . . . fudge. Like flying fudge. Leah crunched her lips together. Crap.

"And?" she tried to restart the conversation.

"You believe." Joshua's voice came out low, without a hint of flirt or irony or that he'd been expecting her to come around.

"I think you have a talent," Leah said. "Some kind of intuition. An ability to compile all the little ticks and trembles we all have and extract a meaning. You think objects help. That's cool. I can go with that. I'm not one of those people who likes to break a painting down to strokes, pigment choice, and perspective. It can take the magic away."

"You want to leave me with my magic," Joshua said.

"I want you to help."

"Me too." Joshua weaved his fingers and bent his wrists backwards, stretching his arms. Warming up for his deal? His pitch? Leah didn't know.

"Boris is torn up inside," Joshua started. "He keeps replaying the scene over and over. The woman walking the dog gets him to turn. The dog pins him, keeps him from putting his attention back where it should be. Not for long, but for long enough. The boy was there, then he wasn't and he hates it. He hates the woman, the dog, and mostly himself. He's lost a step. He has slowed and his years of experience did not make up for it. He got played and he's angry and sad and he prays the little boy is alive. He doesn't think there's a God but if there is, he wants Him to spare the boy."

"You got all that from putting on his sunglasses?" Leah asked.

"Strong emotions," Joshua replied. "They really permeate the material. The glasses were metal, which helps."

"If you're right, it doesn't sound like Boris was an inside man."

Joshua wagged his head slowly.

"If you're right." Leah turned onto Seventh. She regretted it. There had to be a better way downtown. All she needed was one extra brain to figure it out, while her other brain worked on finding Stepan Jr. and another brain tried to figure out Joshua. A third brain. Yep. Not even two would be enough.

"You know I'm right," Joshua said. "You profiled him yourself. You don't fully trust your own talent. I think it let you down in the recent past. It's going to take a while for you to build up some trust in yourself again. You will."

"Is that supposed to be a pep talk?"

"No," Joshua said. "Corroboration. Sympatico. Um . . . backup. I'm backing you up."

"How does yours work?" Leah asked.

"Pardon me?"

"Your talent," Leah blurted. "Your version of intuition. I mean, I'm looking at Boris and thinking this guy is a professional. He keeps his skills up. Stays in shape. He's practiced and serious. He's not the kind of guy to turn, unless Stepan Sr. is such a total monster of an employer he might want revenge."

"He's good to his people," Joshua said.

"Could be," Leah returned. "This doesn't have the scent of revenge anyway. That would have involved extorting large sums of money. Regardless, I know how I came about my information. Observation and reasoning. How about you? What gives you these insights into people through their things?"

They stopped at another intersection. The May light poured into the city now, from a high sun. The bulk of the buildings blocked less when it came straight down. A great day to walk around, shop, go to park, take this guy to a museum and listen to his visions, real or not.

"No idea," Joshua said. He stared out through the side window. Not sulking, exactly. Not admiring the architecture either.

"Sure you do," Leah said. "You've given it a lot of thought. You had to tell Stepan Markov something. He needed a story."

"A story," Joshua repeated. "Sure. I was cursed by a witch because I coveted material goods."

"Not buying it."

"While backpacking in Nepal, I came across a secret monastery dedicated to the arcane practice of Psychometry."

"I think your version of camping is a two star hotel."

"Bitten by a radioactive curator."

"Wow," Leah said. "This is really difficult for you isn't it?"

Joshua shook his head. "Stories are easy."

"The truth is hard."

They looked at each other for two thirds of a second. All that the traffic would allow.

"How does yours work?" Joshua curled his lip on the left.

"Quite nicely, thank you." Leah became riveted by the traffic.

"Your intuition," he continued. "Did you always have a little Nancy Drew in you?"

"No," Leah replied. "Not exactly. I've always loved art. Paintings mostly, but I've come to appreciate everything under the portico."

"That is not the normal path to law enforcement."

"There isn't one," Leah replied. "These paths aren't that divergent, though. I'm still amazed at how much art appreciation and detective work have in common. Motivations, means, opportunity—art, crime, it's all the same thing."

Joshua smiled. "Except artists try to give and criminals take."

"Two sides, same coins." Leah said. "The pros study the coins. Take Van Gogh's sunflower paintings. He wanted to expand his color pallet. More vibrancy. His model doesn't show up and he needs to paint—whether to sell and survive, or because painting is like breathing to him—and all he's got are these enormous flowers. They grow like weeds in Arles. The result is a series of paintings that become icons for him, bitterly loved to this day. Knowing that backstory helps you appreciate them a little bit more, don't you think?"

"I think that's my life's work, really," Joshua said. "I'd love to get my hands on one those sunflower paintings. Literally. The gloves would be off."

"What do you think you'd see?" Leah asked.

"The genius," Joshua replied. "The sad, tortured genius."

"Would you? After more than a hundred years?"

"That's why I like paintings." Joshua spread his gloved hands out. "No one touches them. No one else leaves their impressions. Hundreds of people have put their hands on Michelangelo's *David* since he made his final cut. They leave their own energies behind. Paintings, though. People don't handle those. Not directly."

"Huh," was all she could say. If this man had a screw loose, it certainly was an interesting screw to loose. If he didn't . . . that wasn't for her to decide. Not now, anyway. Later. When she acquired another brain. Or got hers back.

CHAPTER TWENTY SEVEN

"You sure you want to do this?" Leah asked. They sat in the black FBI sedan, half a block down from Joshua's store front home.

"I haven't questioned that for a second," Joshua answered. "Whether this does any good or not . . ."

"We keep moving forward." Leah snapped open the car door.

They got out onto the sidewalk and moved down the block. There were more people moving around than Leah liked to see. Per usual. This town always had more people moving about than seemed right. Did these people have jobs? They weren't all tourists or in-dependently wealthy or searching for a lost child. Why the hell weren't these people in a cubical, staring at spreadsheets or making a new app or doing a load of laundry? Christ, if she had a Thursday morning free, she'd be switching out her heavy black clothes for her lighter black clothes.

A man stood in front of Joshua's "Hats Blocked Here" window. Stocky, five-seven, not quite one-seventy-five, jeans skinny enough to show off his time in the gym. Driving moccasins. A white checked shirt. Matched the pocket square in his medium blue jacket. The man dressed liked two-thirds of the males at any given spring show. She would not need an introduction.

"Neal." Joshua put his hands behind his back and made a brief bow.

"Joshua." Neal Pozner smiled and bowed in response. "And this is?"

Leah held out her hand. "Special Agent Leah Capello. FBI. We spoke on the phone." She watched his face. Neal's mouth held it's smile, but the amusement left his eyes.

"Certainly." Neal shook her hand with care.

"So glad you could stop by." Joshua passed them and unlocked his front door.

Neal said nothing as Joshua fiddled with the door. Leah didn't feel like helping him out. None of them were in the mood for small talk. Leah knew everyone wanted to get to the big stuff. She followed the boys inside and to the left. Joshua flicked the lights on, giving her a much better look at the collection than she'd seen the night before. She could've spent the next four days sifting through it all, lifting the drapes, opening the drawers, trying to identify some of the *objects d'art* that lay outside her expertise.

The Bacon painting stood where she remembered, set like a jewel in the vice of the studio easel. A reclining figure of man, naked, pale, pulled like taffy. Leah loved it.

Joshua took a position next to the piece. Neal got within a foot and stopped, arms crossed. His head scanned slowly, as if he were reading it. He asked if he could see the back. Joshua unscrewed the top bar, lifted the painting out and flipped it around. After moment, he spun it back and leaned onto the easel.

"There is a phrase," Neal said. "Too good to be true."

"It's in the new cat res," Joshua returned.

"Really?"

"As real as the deal."

"It doesn't make any sense to me."

"Does it need to?"

Neal glanced at Leah, the corners of his mouth plunging. Leah kept her face blank. Broadway did not offer as much theatre as the art world. While Broadway shows ran up to eight times a week, art deals were done hundreds of times a day, everywhere—everyone hiding an emotion, exaggerating a feeling, posturing, praying, weeping and wringing hands. The net effect: Leah believed very little of what she saw in the course of a negotiation. In this case, she didn't believe Neal had any reservations, no matter how much he stretched out this moment, or how contemplative he made himself appear.

"This list of mine," Neal said. "It contains the most resource-intensive clients in the city, maybe the world. Their privacy expectations are exceptionally high. If it becomes known that I gave this list out, I would lose a precious commodity: their trust. Once you lose that, it is almost impossible to get back."

"We're not asking you to betray anyone's trust." Joshua lowered his head a half-inch and smiled without parting his lips. They rippled. He batted his eyes and whispered, without breaking his grin, "No one's going to know."

Works for me, Leah thought. It should work for Neal, too. Even if he were straight, that smile would work on him. Just keep quiet. Just keep quiet. Let Joshua do his thing.

Neal reached to an inside jacket pocket. He pulled out a piece of paper, folded like a letter. He passed it to Joshua, pinched between his first and second fingers. "I hope you find what you're looking for."

"Thank you very much." Joshua took the paper, handed it to Leah and turned to the painting. "Let me wrap this up for you."

Joshua took two steps over to a large, gray drafting table. A roll of brown butcher paper hung on a spit at the top. He pulled a yard of it down.

Leah opened the paper. Computer print on white, eight-and-a-half by eleven. She read it as Joshua packaged the painting.

Rohan Kavanagh

Stepan Markov

Li Lau

Emerson Bly

Marcella Alvaro

Oscar Pierce

Lac Khor

Hazlitt Demir

She recognized four names on the list, but felt she may have heard each of the names at some point in her past. Stepan and Oscar, obviously. Rohan Kavanagh was a hedge fund manager with a hundred acres of art in Connecticut. Marcella Alvaro was the second richest wo-man in the world. She'd need to jumpstart her memory for the others.

"I'll let you know next time I'm having a private auction." Neal turned, brown paper package under his arm. "Perhaps you'll want that list, too."

Leah stared at Neal's smirk. He strained to contain it. He could barely keep his smile from pulling his face apart, like some . . . well . . . Francis Bacon portrait.

167

She felt rolled, twisted and bunted up herself. No smile though. She jammed her lips together until she heard the door close and click.

"What a tool," she blurted.

"He's just making a deal," Joshua responded. "That's what he does."

"He doesn't have to be such a tool about it."

"May I see the list?"

Leah handed it to him. She watched his face as he read it. Blank. He put his left hand in his mouth and pulled off the glove. He pressed his hand to the paper and closed his eyes. He flipped the paper over and traced one small circle with his palm. He opened his eyes, dropped the glove from his mouth back to his left hand and said, "He's nervous."

"About what?" Leah asked.

"I can't tell. He only handled the paper for a moment."

"Tonight is a big deal for him," Leah said. "Some people's blood pressure rises when they hear FBI."

"I can't imagine if you were hot on my tail."

Leah rolled her eyes.

"What time is it?" Joshua asked.

Leah looked at her tiny, silver watch. "Ten after twelve."

"Eight hours," Joshua said. "Lots of time."

"To what?"

"Pay visits."

CHAPTER TWENTY EIGHT

Leah's first gallery job, back while she still worked on her Masters of Science in History of Art and Design, was at Cocoon Two. For reasons Leah never figured out, Magdalena Brown took a liking to her. Magdalena paid her to stand around, answer questions, fetch her if things got interesting, and, most importantly, figure out *when* things got interesting. It was not always apparent in a gallery. Millionaires looked like bums, bums looked like artists, artists looked like skate punks, because they were skate punks, even though a few would have been better off practicing their grinds and slides than trying to be the next Keith Haring.

A professor had sent Leah to see Magdalena, who proceeded to walk around her as she might a medium-sized installation she considered acquiring. She put her face close to Leah's and asked her to smile and keep smiling until she asked her to stop. She pointed to a wide oil paint-ing hanging at the far wall. She asked Leah what she thought of it. Really. Just between the two of them.

Leah looked at the waves of thick, stringy colors. Reds, oranges and yellows, descending into greens and blues.

"Pleasant, but simple," Leah said. "The artist knows how to apply oil paints and evoke a sunset over the ocean, but, you know, sunsets are already pretty. There is nothing else here. A reproduction of what's already pretty, and failing the real thing. To be honest."

"It's colorful and fits nicely over a sofa," Magdalena said. "I bought it for $800, I'll sell it for $2,000 for a profit of $1,200 probably by next week. Everyone's happy. You'll see. You'll be fine, darling. You start in two days, no?"

Leah said "yes" in what she often looked back on as her last solidly great decision. So it gave her a slight—very slight—feeling of comfort to walk back in to Cocoon Two now. At the entrance, a new and improved gallery girl—ten years younger, twenty pounds lighter, two shades darker on the skin tone chart at the Bobbi Brown counter, making it appear that the young lady actually got out in the sun sometimes—smiled equally at Leah and Joshua as they entered. Smart.

"Hello," the young lady started.

And stopped. Magdalena came out of the back like a frizzy black explosion, arms raised, fingers splayed—the unfamiliar might assume she was throwing a curse or scaring bats.

"Daaaaaarling," she made last from the office to the embrace. Leah hugged her back. As they parted, Magdalena gave Joshua the up and down. "What did you bring me? My goodness."

"My friend," Leah said.

"Sure, darling. Sure." Magdalena held out her hand.

Joshua kissed the air just above the back and introduced himself. Magdalena swooned. Leah grimaced and urged them all into the back office. A cramped, cluttered, minor warehouse, Leah knew where everything was, because none of it had moved in the five years since she'd been gone. It had two gray steel chairs with jade green faux leather tops and backs. She urged Joshua to take one, she the other and let Magdalena move behind her battleship desk.

Leah put up her hand, hoping she could block Magdalena's inner torrent for the five minutes she needed, and poured out everything she wanted the woman to know. The kidnapping, the secret art deal, Neal Pozner and his list. She left out Joshua's more interesting bits.

"That is the worst thing I've ever heard," Magdalena said. "The worst. I have a heard a lot, let me tell you. I don't have to tell you. A little boy."

"Here's the list." Leah handed it to her. "We think someone on this list took the Markov child."

Magdalena held it as far as her arm allowed and squinted at the type.

"You say you spoke with Pierce already," Magdalena said.

"He was like you said," Leah replied.

"A tall pile of shit. Who thinks he's not. I like better the people who know they are shit and live with it."

Joshua smiled. "Not everyone knows themselves that well."

"You're a young man," Magdalena said. "When you are Pierce's age, you should have an understanding. Rohan Kavanagh—you know him, darling."

Leah said, "We've met."

"He's a Buddhist. He likes to say that, anyway. But it's not true and I know this because he's the richest God damned Buddhist in the world, which is easy because none of them are supposed to be rich. To me, he is a fraud. A fraud with exquisite taste. He's been in here, you know."

"I know," Leah said.

Magdalena looked at Joshua. "He has come in here because he looks for the next new thing. He buys Picassos, sure, but he buys fresh, too. I don't know that he could take a child. Who could, really? He's a fraud, that's all I can say."

"Marcella Alvaro," Joshua said. "Has she been in here?"

"She is not like Kavanagh. She likes the names that everyone knows. With her money, she can be that way. I don't care. Who am I to judge? I don't know what I'd be like with her kind of money. Her kind of money puts you in a different world."

"The kind that makes kidnapping an acceptable bargaining ploy?" Leah asked.

Magdalena shrugged. "When you are the center of the world, things like that mater less, no?"

"No," Leah said.

"Emerson Bly and his wife have a wonderful post-modernist collection. He made his money the old fashioned way. I've met them twice. They are not as interesting as their acquisitions."

"Lac Khor," Joshua said.

"He is new," Magdalena returned. "I have never had the pleasure of meeting the man. He is from Taiwan and only travels to this city when there is something magnificent happening. He is the second name on this list that makes me want to be invited to this event tonight. If he is in town the slate must be very ripe. Deliciously so ripe. I wonder—"

"Who's first?" Leah interrupted.

"Li Lau," Magdalena said. "I have no idea who that is. I don't have to tell you that I know everyone. If this Li Lau person is going tonight, I want to be there."

"Wherever that is," Joshua said.

Leah asked, "Hazlitt Demir?"

"Oh, that bastard," Magdalena answered. "He'd burn down an orphanage to find a half-finished De Kooning."

Leah sat back, folded her arms across her chest and huffed. Joshua put his arm over the back of his chair, interlocked his white-gloved fingers and looked at Magdalena.

"Who took the boy?" he asked.

Magdalene ran her eyes down the list again, mouth like a prune. "No one trades a little boy for art. So that means anyone can."

Leah took the list and smoothed it flat to the desk.

"I feel like I should know you," Magdalene said to Joshua.

"I try to keep off the stage," he returned.

Leah took out her phone, photographed the list and sent it to Dean with the subject line reading: Need current locations of these people.

"You seem nice enough," Magdalena said. "In this business, everything is not always what it seems."

Joshua made a sliver of a smile. "That has been my distinct experience."

"You're in the business. I thought so. Good."

Dean texted back. Leah read his question mark and she replied with an "explanation to follow."

Magdalena leaned over the desk, low to get as close to Joshua as the furniture would allow. "If you break her heart, I'll see to it you never put foot in a gallery in this city ever again. Even the public ones, I get you banned."

Joshua put his forearms on the desk and leaned to within an inch of Magdalena's head. "And if she breaks mine?"

Magdalena said, "That's her business."

CHAPTER TWENTY NINE

Leah and Joshua exited the Cocoon Two. The air had a pleasant warmth, the newborn spring kind, not yet full of the rancid staleness the city would soon bake. The exploitive bake of the summer. She liked the city best in the spring or the fall when the place didn't feel like a pizza oven that hadn't been cleaned since the boys brought the idea back from fighting in the big one.

"Turn around." A woman's voice, from behind. Leah thought she'd heard it before. Possibly. She certainly didn't care for the tone.

She spun, ready to say something which failed in her mouth. Marisa. Joshua's friend from the hotel yesterday. The woman leaned back against the wall, knee sticking out through the part in her trench coat, obviously trying to recreate a film noir poster.

"I don't have any cigarettes," Leah said.

"What are you doing here?" Joshua used a schoolteacher voice. Not threatening, not happy.

"She's got a mouth on her." Marisa stared at Leah. "But really, that's about it."

Totally the wrong time of day for the whole pulp fiction look, Leah thought. Really. It doesn't work at lunchtime.

"We're not together," Joshua said.

"Don't give me that, Josh. She spent the night at your place."

"You're stalking me?"

"Alright," Leah said. "I don't have time to arrest you right now, so run along before you make it impossible not to."

"I'm not the one who's going to be running, sweetheart." Marisa poked a thumb into the belt of her trench and pulled it loose. The coat fell away, revealing a tasteful black and white poke-a-dot dress. A little short, but she took her flirting seriously. As evidenced by the strap of batteries, wires and what looked like two bricks of gray, plastic-wrapped lard.

"That belt goes with, well, nothing really," Leah said.

Four feet, Leah thought. A tad too far.

"Christ, Marisa," Joshua said. "What is that?"

"Explosives," Marisa answered.

"I don't think so," Leah said.

"Where would you get explosives?" Joshua asked.

"Jersey," Marisa answered.

"Cinch up your coat," Leah demanded. Two women were walking down the sidewalk from the east. A man came from the west. "None of us want to make this a big scene, right?"

Marisa drew her coat together, keeping her right hand inside the folds, using the left to keep the folds tight to her body.

"And this is accomplishing what, exactly?" Joshua put his hands on his hips, and cocked his head to the right. Like his dog had taken yet another crap on his carpet.

"Your little fling is going to walk one way. You and I are going to walk the other. And nobody gets hurt."

"Put your hands where I can seem them," Leah ordered.

"My hand stays on the button."

The two women sauntered between them. Another day in the Big Apple. None of them spoke until the women passed.

Leah said, "Not that this should need to be said, but you can't be with Joshua if you blow him up."

"Neither can you."

"This is silly," Joshua said. "Go home. I'll call you tomorrow."

"Silly!" Marisa sneered. "You think my love for you is silly?"

"No," Leah cut in. "This particular expression of your love is silly."

"I don't need to hear from you right now."

"Why?" Leah sneered back. "'Cuz you've got the modeling clay?"

"Don't push me."

The man walked around them. Bobbing his head to whatever played through his headphones. Leah glanced up and down again. Another woman twelve paces behind headphone guy. Two men coming from the other direction.

Try to open a channel on her phone, let Dean listen in, figure out the problem and send in the tactical squad? Time consuming. Draw and shoot this chick in the head? Hope she doesn't have time to push her button? Risky. Let Joshua leave with her and get some help? Letting a suicide bomber out of your sight could not be the right play.

"What kind of explosives do you have?" Leah crossed her arms.

"I told you not to speak," Marisa returned.

"No need to be rude," Joshua said.

Pedestrians approached. They would forever and ever.

"She's being rude." Marisa kept her eyes on Leah. "I asked her to leave."

Phone in her left breast pocket. Sunglasses in the right.

"Fine," Leah said. "It's just, you know, if the stuff is real, you should know what it is."

Two men, gabbing away, moved to pass between them all. Joshua and Leah had to back up a step. Marisa made a 'c' by cupping her hands, then held up four fingers.

Leah held up one finger as the woman passed. She returned her arms to crossing across her chest. She plunged her left hand into her right breast pocket, took her sunglasses and flung them at Marisa.

Marisa raised both hands to catch them. Leah lunged, grabbing the woman's wrists and slamming her back against the wall of Cocoon Two. She dipped her hip, brought her right leg behind Marisa's and straightened up. Marisa lost her footing. Leah twisted her to the ground.

"Bitch!" Marisa shouted.

Leah straddled her.

"Get off me, you bitch!"

"Joshua," Leah said.

"Got it." He dashed towards them.

Leah looked down at Marisa as her face bulged and went scarlet. She wrenched and torqued and got no leverage. Leah said, "Stop it." Marisa didn't.

Joshua said, "Mod Podge."

"What?" Leah asked.

"It's crafting crap."

"Your sure?"

"I'd bet my life on it."

Leah reached back, took out her handcuffs and snapped one ring onto Marisa's right wrist. She leaned back, yanked and used the momentum to roll her over. Then she clicked the other, securing Marisa's hands behind her back.

"Josh," Marisa cried. "You love me. I know you love me."

"I knew you were going to get me to arrest you," Leah said. "I just knew it. Shit, crap, fuck, now I've got to take you to One." She stood and helped Marisa to her feet. "I've got lots to do today. Lots way more important than processing you, you know?" She pushed Marisa face-first into the wall and looked over at Joshua. He pulled his right glove back on.

"Josh," Marisa whimpered. "Tell her. Tell her I'd never hurt you. This was a stunt. A joke, right? I do crazy things because I'm crazy about you."

"I think she figured that out." Joshua brushed the knees of his jeans. "She's clever that way."

CHAPTER THIRTY

Leah used the rearview mirror to glance at Marisa. She sat in back, melting her face in to such a frown it must have hurt.

"Why can't he sit back here with me?" Marisa asked.

"Because I don't like you." Leah pulled away from the curve. "It's personal."

"Sorry about this," Joshua said, head back against the screen separating the front seats from the back.

"Not your fault," Leah said.

"It is."

"Where are you taking me?" Marisa whined. "Is it a crime to wear a belt of Mod Podge?"

"With that outfit?" Leah said. "Totally. A felony."

"Are we going to FBI Headquarters?" Joshua watched out the side window.

"I don't see much of a choice." Leah stopped at the first light, ran her hands back through her hair and tightened her ponytail. "And from there, the day is shot. It will take a couple of hours to process her. Paperwork, though it's not much on paper. Which isn't even the problem.

Dean's had me labeled as sketchy since this morning. He knows I've giving him three-tenths of a story. He's a good agent. A good friend. Once he's got me in the flesh, he's going to wring all the truth he can out of me."

"Can't we explain to him we're in a hurry?"

"Number one," Leah said, "there's no 'we'. You're what I might call a question multiplier. You know? He'll take one look at you and keep us around all night. Second, he'll really want to know what's more pressing that than the Claymation bombshell I just brought in. That story isn't going to make anyone's afternoon better."

"You should let me go," Marisa said.

Leah again looked into the rearview mirror. "You're a crazy-ass bitch who probably would've used a real C4 strap-on if you could've gotten your hands on one."

"I'd never."

"If you asked me to hose you down because you were on fire, I wouldn't believe you." Leah sped up to the next light, stopped, thought about turning on the lights and sirens, and thought better of it. She needed a few moments in the seat. Even if it meant Manhattan traffic and being two feet from Miss Bridge Mix for an extra ten minutes.

"Can you drop me at my place?"

"No," Marisa howled from the back. "I'm so scared. Please, Josh, please."

"Why?" Leah asked.

"Because," Joshua said, "I serve no purpose sitting around downtown."

"I need you there!" Marisa barked.

Leah agreed with her, though she attributed the pronoun a little more personally.

Marisa said, "Don't let me get arrested alone."

Joshua turned around to face Marisa. "There is nothing I can do for you right now. Nothing. I'm sorry. I wish to God there was, but there's not."

"But you're the center of my world." Marisa's voice cracked. Leah didn't have to look back to know the sobbing would begin soon. Real, authentic sobbing.

"I won't press charges," he said. "I'll speak on your behalf. I'll make sure you get a lawyer and help. We'll—"

"Help!" she screamed. "I don't need help! I need you! If you'd stayed with me, none of this ever would have happened. Not Monday. Not today. None of this."

"I know," Joshua said. "That's why I'll get you—"

"Don't." Marisa said through clenched teeth. "Don't. You. Say. It."

The exchange did not help Leah's thinking. She'd bent so many rules, policies and procedures in the last two days one more push and it would all snap. All of it.

"You can't work this list on your own," she said, trying the weave the car through solid traffic.

"I've got options," Joshua said.

"Name one."

"I can't talk about it here."

"That's what I thought," Leah said.

"Maybe I can visit one or two," Joshua said. "Touch a few things. Learn something. At the very least, I could narrow the field of suspects."

"If you found the right one you'd wind up dead."

"Dead?" Marisa chirped from the back.

"Isn't that what we were going to do?" Joshua asked.

"That's what I was going to do." Leah did not look at him. She didn't get the feeling that he looked at her either. They both stared out into the sheer steel valley of stuttered movement, refracted light and contorted reflections. She could see them both, their faces in tones of black and silver, ghosting in the back window of the SUV in front of them. They looked pale and lost, like they sat in purgatory, awaiting instructions, stunned and numb. A heavy black frame around a glass. A mixed media piece—film negative and acrylics. *Nowhere to Turn*, she named it.

Nope. Not today. She had somewhere to turn—on to West 11th, into the Village. She drove down the narrow, leafy lane, lined with cars on each side, chunky charms in cast-off bracelets. Red and browns brick buildings with warm gray of the stoops. Pots of azaleas and hostas. The whole neighborhood felt like a corner bedroom, on a day when everyone else had school.

She parked the car next to a fire hydrant, turned it off and pulled the door release.

"What are you doing?" Joshua pushed open his door. He looked across the pond of glossy black steel for a response.

"I haven't decided yet." Leah came around the car. "I was taught not to rush investigations. Take the time you need to get things right. So you know what?" She opened the back door and reached in for Marisa. "That's what I'm going to do."

"You're letting me go?" Marisa crunched and wriggled out of the car.

"Hell, no." Leah got behind her and urged her towards the door to Joshua's brownstone. "I'm just not taking you in right now."

Joshua skipped ahead and performed the various procedures required to open his door. Marisa led the way up the stairs. Leah kept her hand on the chain of the handcuffs. Joshua closed his door and followed. Back in the living room, Leah told Marisa to sit and be very quiet. She took the paper Neal Pozner had given them. No. Sold them for nearly a million dollars worth of art. She went up to the far wall with its single nail angled up, suggestively, she thought, and thought again. She slammed the list onto the nail like Luther at the chapel door. She took off her jacket and nestled into the crux of the sofa, arm over the back.

"Make yourself at home," Joshua said.

"Sorry," Leah said. "I'm thinking."

"These handcuffs are killing me." Marisa sat on the edge one of the tweed chairs.

"Then you shouldn't threaten to blow people up," Leah re-turned.

"What are you thinking about?" Joshua slunk into the other tweed chair.

"That we're going about this all wrong," Leah said. "There are two ways to catch prey. Chase it down—that's what we've been doing since last night, and I'm starting to think we're going to run out of time. Or trap it. You remember the first time we met?"

"I'll never forget it," Joshua said.

Marisa sat up straight. "Do you remember the first time *we* met?"

"God, girl," Leah huffed. "Give it up, alright? We're not reminiscing about two straws and a malt, OK? We're discussing a crime."

"Your discussion is a crime," Marisa said.

"Do I have to gag you? Because I will. With a ball of fresh mozzarella. You ever been gagged with a ball of fresh mozzarella? I'm not talking about a block of some shit from Krogers. I'm talking fresh pulled from Vito's down on Ninth that will take on the shape of your mouth for three hours. Is that what you want?"

Marisa stared at her. "Are you really an FBI agent?"

"Are you still talking?"

"Soooo," Joshua jumped in. "About this trap business."

Leah settled back into the chair. "Traps. Right. Anyway, we could traipse all over the city between now and eight, hoping to catch a break. Or we could wait until everyone gathers in one place and make our own."

Joshua looked up at the list on the wall. He pressed the fingers of his gloved hands together, making a little five-barred trap of his own. "That's cutting it a bit close, don't you think?"

"Down to the wire," Leah returned.

They both gazed at the list. Art on a wall, to be considered. Absorbed. Mulled over, pulled apart and reconstructed.

"You're not contemplating a sting," Joshua said. "This would be a con."

"You in?"

Joshua said, "For a pound."

CHAPTER THIRTY ONE

Leah got up from the sofa and got her phone out. She would need some help tonight and had recently met just the right people to supply it.

"Scott?" she said into the phone as it was answered. "Thanks for taking my call."

"Curiosity beat my better judgment to death," he replied.

"I'm getting the old gang back together. Right now, if it's convenient. And I'm only saying that second part to be nice. I really need you, Dani, Van and Asuna for a performance tonight."

There was a healthy pause on the other end of the call. Then he said, "That is going to be problematic."

"Do you need help solving any of these problems?"

"I don't know how interested my friends are in coming in on their own recognizance."

"That's not it. I need you all for something different."

"Is it legal?"

"It's performance art. One night only."

Another pause. "Let me do some texting."

"Excellent." Leah gave him the address and pressed the red button on her phone. "Your turn," she said to Joshua.

Joshua thumbed over his phone and brought it up to his ear. "Lidiya?" He listened for a few seconds. "We have an idea of sorts. Special Agent Capello and me. How do you feel about popping over and discussing it?" He waited again, eyes on Leah. "Here's the thing, though. Ah. Could you not tell Stepan just yet? You know how he is. Especially today." He listened for too long, Leah thought. Too long. Finally he smiled and thanked her and ended the call. "She's on her way."

Leah moved her mouth around. Not quite a smile, not quite a frown. A cheek exercise. She decided she had no natural expression for nervous relief and gave up. She went for flat, business as usual, blankness. Like she directed criminal enterprises everyday.

Joshua went off into his bedroom.

Marisa luxuriated across the couch as if preparing for a photo shoot. Cute little polka dot dress, handcuffs, bomb and detonator belt. Leah decided some of it had to go before company arrived.

"I'm going to remove those cuffs," she said. "And you are going to behave yourself."

Marisa's mouth curved up at the ends. She blinked slowly. "Of course."

Leah opened the handcuffs and tucked them back into the belt-pouch near the small of her back. Then she asked for the belt. Marisa put her arms up and looked off to the bedroom door, after Joshua. She never let her eyes stray too far from him, Leah noticed. Ever. Leah put the belt on the coffee table and stood staring down at Marisa. Fit. Pretty. She wanted to say 'smart', but the woman's wackiness got in the way. Was that

Joshua's type? Thin, attractive nut-jobs? Had she hid the nuttiness at first? Until it was too late? Or didn't he care until it was too late?

Men.

Leah took out her phone again and stepped to the side. She brought up a recent call and pressed the name.

"Hello?" The woman's voice from this morning, with the faint accent she couldn't identify.

"It's the FBI again, for Mr. Pierce."

"Oh."

"He's got the number and if you could tell him it was a matter of some urgency, I would be very thankful."

"Certainly."

They ended the call together.

"So where did you and Joshua meet?" Marisa asked.

"A hotel." Leah stood, phone in hand, waiting for the buzz of a return call.

"Out trolling for little action?" Marisa continued.

"That is kind of my job."

"He'll be done with you soon."

"What's that supposed to mean?" Leah asked.

"When this adventure is over," Marisa said. "This crime you keep talking about. He'll get tired of it soon and toss you aside, like all that crap on the first floor. Prepare to be another artifact."

"Exactly how long have you—" Leah's phone vibrated in her hand. She humpfed and brought it up to her ear.

"Special Agent Capello."

"You called?" Oscar Pierce asked.

"I need the time and location for tonight's event."

"I take it you're not on the invite list."

"It got lost in the mail," Leah said.

Pierce said, "It's a secret."

"Because it's shady," she returned. "But you're not shady. You don't want to be involved in stolen goods or illicit trafficking. You are above that kind of thing. Still, you want to go, right? And if it does turn out that tonight's feature item is less than legal, you might want to say you knew it all along and that's why you've working with the proper authorities."

"And if it's not? If everything's up and up?"

"Then we can enjoy a glass of Cristal together."

Pierce chuckled. "You drive an easy bargain. I'll have Vita text you."

"Cheers."

He chuckled again as he hung up.

Leah lowered her phone and returned her attention to Marisa. She thought about resuming their conversation and then thought some more. She needed her brain on other things.

Joshua returned, clapped his ungloved hands together and asked, "Can I get anyone anything?"

"Cosmo," Marisa said.

"Make it . . ." Leah started, stopped and said, "water."

"Right." He spun into his kitchen.

Leah sat down and gazed into her phone until a text came in, from Vita. It read: 8:00 PM. The Printers Union. Room 1001. She didn't know the place, which was fine. She welcomed the chance to dive into some deep research. Plan, scheme, do something productive. Or terribly destructive, depending on how things turned out.

Joshua brought her some water. She brought up the hotel's website. A boutique hotel, on Lafayette, in Nolita. A neighborhood she didn't visit. She knew the building, though. It had an enormous 'P' and 'U' at the corner, type-set letters, if you needed your font size in the thousands. The building had been once been the home of a printer's guild and famous two centuries ago for producing satirical magazines. Now it housed the chic and snarky for five-hundred a night.

She called and inquired about facilities for a small party. Maybe twenty-five people. They said the tenth floor had been laid out for exactly that kind of gathering. It was, of course, booked for tonight.

Joshua set the glass of water down on a small table next to her and bent in over her shoulder. "What's the venue like?"

"Sultry," she said.

"As it should be." He lingered. She could feel his breath on the back of her neck, just behind her ear.

"Is anyone else a little peckish?" Marisa asked, with more volume than Leah thought necessary. "Should we order out?"

Joshua stood. "It's getting to be about that time."

Leah looked up from her phone and directly at Marisa. "Maybe you could whip something up. A nice casserole. Maybe a pie."

Marisa said, "I left my apron and pearls back at the hotel."

Leah returned to her phone. She flipped through the hotel's photo gallery trying to get a sense of the layout. The smart thing would have been to run over there. It wasn't that far. The really smart thing would have been calling her supervising agent and setting this thing up right and proper. None of which fit her tastes at the moment. She had to keep this lean and mean. It was a deal. The fewer people involved the better. Way fewer than the Bureau would bring in.

"How about Thai?" Joshua asked.

"Fabulous," Marisa replied.

"Sure," Leah said, wondering if she'd be able to keep anything down until sometime tomorrow.

CHAPTER THIRTY TWO

"That is absurd," Lidiya Markov said. She looked over at Boris, standing by the door, arms at his sides. He shook his head, keeping his eyes on Leah. Which she liked. His instincts told him she was the most dangerous person in the room. He'd underestimated Marisa, but, anyway, she'd take the compliment.

Lidiya sat on the couch, next to Joshua. Leah had one of the chairs. They'd sent Marisa into the kitchen where she perched on a café stool, ears wide, mouth closed, eyes ever on Joshua. She sipped her second cosmo. Another thing Leah liked. Maybe the chick would get sleepy.

"I know it's odd," Joshua said.

"You said you had an idea. This is not a good one."

"I agree completely," Leah agreed. "It's downright crazy."

"Then why are you asking me this?" Lidiya asked. "I'm no actor. I do not play at parts. I do not play at anything."

"It's our only idea." Leah moved to the edge of her seat. "If I had anything else, anything, I'd use it. I wouldn't involve you or anyone else and especially not this nonsense. The fact is, you can't fight math." Leah pointed to the list on the wall above Lidiya. She turned to see it. Leah continued, "I don't know who in that group has your son. I don't have time to deal with them individually, so I'm going to deal with them as a whole."

Lidiya turned back. "It is dangerous."

"I think it's less dangerous than doing nothing."

"You would bet my son's life on that?"

"No," Leah said. "I'm asking you to."

Lidiya swallowed. Her eyes sparkled in the prelude of tears. Leah sat back, exhaling without making a show of it. She didn't want anyone thinking her frustrated or annoyed. She just needed to breathe more. Lots more. Tons more. At the park, in the sun.

"The talent is not something I have," Lidiya said. "I'm not thinking I can do this."

"I can." The voice came from the door. They all turned to look at Boris. Even Marisa got off her stool to peak around and see there the low two syllables of distant thunder originated. "It will be believable from me, because I would blow all the fucking bastards up to get little Stepan back."

Everyone stared.

Boris walked in between the tweed chairs and picked up Marisa's belt. The fake detonator switch swung from thin red wires. He tapped one of the two Mod Podge-doctored blocks with his middle finger.

"This shit is fake," he said. "I will need two hours to get real explosives."

"No, no," Leah and Joshua said together.

"Fake is fine," Leah continued.

"Love fakes," Joshua added. "My life is fakes."

Boris weighed the belt in his hands. "C4 is much heavier. If would be more believable if I had the real thing."

"This group won't know the difference," Leah said.

"You are convincing all by yourself," Joshua said.

Boris looked at Lidiya.

"I can't ask you do to this," she said.

"There is no asking," he replied. "I'm off tonight. This is my thing."

"It's too dangerous."

"Actually not," Boris said. "It is stupid and will never work. So not much danger. You stay with Mr. Markov tonight. I will get little Stepan."

Lidiya put her hand to her mouth and looked down.

"Come," Boris said. "I'll take you home." Boris threw the belt over his shoulder and turned to Leah. "You can send Mrs. Markov the time and place. I will be there. I will know what to do."

"No real explosives," Leah said.

Boris met her eyes with his, large, sad and steady. "No."

Lidiya got up. Joshua gave her a brief hug. She and Boris left.

"Now him I like," Marisa said from the kitchen.

CHAPTER THIRTY THREE

"I don't give a damn about the art."

Dean told her three years ago that it was all about the people. He had been assigned to her case and came out to The Wen to interview her. He asked her a lot of questions about Archibald Lee. She told him everything she could, pulled the video from the gallery's surveillance system and got the faux Turner out of the vault. He had no interest in the painting.

"It's a forgery," he said. "Why would I have any interest in it?"

Leah didn't remember exactly what she said. Something about it being a clue or evidence. Her statement didn't stick with her.

Dean's statement stuck. "This is about people." Dean informed her. "It's always about the people."

He'd said 'people', the plural, not 'person', as in Archibald Lee. He meant the gallery owner mattered, the painter mattered, and Leah came to realize that she mattered, too. Her recent promotion from gallerina to sales made her naïve and hungry. The perfect mark. The perfect fool. Finally, she was perfect at something and it had to be patsy, right?

Nope.

"The painting matters, too," Leah had insisted. "It's like a person. It has a look and feel. It even has a smell. Put it to your nose. The canvas has a scent that is, as far as I know, impossible to fake. So this guy went through the trouble of finding aged material. In terms of technique, the forgery is masterful. Whoever did this is a gifted painter in his or her own right. Its theme is very revealing. The sunset and swirl allude to the fact that something's not right, right under the surface. This is both a joke and a con. The artist is having fun, and—given the modest amount he took from us—I bet fun is more than half the reason he pulled this scam. He's probably done this before and he's certainly going to do it again."

"The painting talks to you, huh," Dean said.

"Like a person."

"Does it make you mad? The crime?"

"You have no idea. I'll do whatever it takes. The guy is not getting away."

"You ever think of changing your career path?"

"No," Leah said, "But my boss might be having those thoughts."

Motive to motivation. Putting things in motion.

People. Leah studied the list on the wall of Joshua's apartment, waiting for it to speak to her. She got a buzz from the street door instead.

Scott, Dani, Asuna, and Van skittered into the living room as if it were a haunted house, as if something might jump out, or cant forward, or spin, whirl or drop two stories. Leah felt bad for them, because what she had planned would be real and much more scary.

"Cool place," Van said as he sat down on the couch.

"This ain't a party," Asuna snarled. She sat on the arm of the couch, glaring at Leah.

"Party-ish." Joshua clapped his gloved hands together. "I have beer, wine, a pretty outlandish bar, not to brag."

The boys and Dani agreed to beer. Asuna wanted water. Joshua hopped into the kitchen. Leah directed Scott and Dani to the couch, stood in the middle of the room and said, "I need you all for another job."

"No," came from Asuna

"What do you mean 'another'?" Dani said.

Van asked, "Does it pay?"

Scott leaned forward, arms on his knees, hands clasped together. "We make people laugh. That's what we do. We improvise comedy in situ, ad hoc—"

"Tempus Fugit," Van added.

"Caveat emptor," Dani said.

"Covet the what?" Scott spun.

"Unum, I think. E pluribus."

"Does the E pluribus get me up-town?"

"Naw, you want the F pluribus for that," Van said.

"Or *you*—" Dani started singing, a sustained note, waiting for the others to join in. Van added his voice, then Scott. They all looked at Asuna. She shook her head, frowning deeply. The trio got louder. Van nudged her with his elbow.

Asuna raised her head and sang, "*Must take the A train, To go to Sugar Hill way up in Harlem.*"

Scott snapped an upturned hand in front of his face. "Scene."

All four bowed slightly.

"That's what we do," Scott said.

Marisa clapped from the island in the kitchen. Leah smirked. Joshua entered, three longneck beer bottles in one hand, dangling like glass utters. He had a tall glass of water in the other, slice of lemon rising from the rim.

"Is that what you want us to do tonight?" Scott took his beer.

"Teamwork, thinking on your feet, cleverness," Leah said. "Yep. That'll do it."

"But we won't," Scott said.

"You don't even know what it is," Leah returned.

"You didn't call us to do a Quinceañera. You didn't call us down to FBI headquarters. You want to use us for some off-the-books, probably illegal activity that we don't want to do. And I'm thinking we don't have to, because you can't threaten us with prosecution to make us do something else we can be prosecuted for."

"Huh." Leah looked at Joshua. He popped his eyebrows and sat down in one of the tweed chairs. "Then what are you doing here?" Leah asked.

Scott's eyes fixed. He knew how to hide his emotions. Van pointed his head towards the kitchen. He no longer wanted to be in the room. Asuna's mouth cinched closed, like she had a drawstring hemmed into her lips. Dani cranked her head back and opened her mouth. Leah thought she might be praying. Or about to toss a Cheeto in the air and try and catch it.

Dani lowered her head. "Is this about the little boy?"

"It is," Leah replied.

"We're in."

CHAPTER THIRTY FOUR

"What are you humming?" Leah Capello turned the car onto Bleecker Street.

"*Take The 'A' Train,*" Joshua said. "Can't help it. Last song I heard. That Asuna has an excellent voice."

"Stop. It's not helping."

"Which is tragic, me being here to help and all."

"How exactly?" Leah asked. "How are you helping?"

"Billy Strayhorn wrote the *Take the 'A' Train.*" Joshua snuggled into his seat, faced forward and flopped his arms wide. His left hand came within a few inches of Leah's upper leg. The white glove lay open, like a lily. "I held a manuscript by him once. I'd hoped to get a glimpse inside the composer's head. A musical genius is interesting, but a black man, openly gay, making a living in the music business in the 1940s? He must have been very special. I took those pages and pressed them be-tween my hands and I saw a flash of him, of his feeling. He gushed out excitement when he'd gotten a certain bar just right. When it worked. It was like falling in love, a little, his creative process. That was it, though. Just a one frame of a long film.

"Which is why I don't collect manuscripts. Partly because other people touch them and whiten the noise. But also because writers and composers don't labor over the physical medium for long. Sometimes—some poets—but it's rare. Not like painters. They can pump hours and hours of emotion into a single square inch. That's what you want to tap into, to drink. To take a work of beauty in your hands and brush your fingers along the surface, feathering the swells and valleys, the perfections, letting them gently tip you into a well of feelings, letting you live an-other's sensations, the restlessness, the rush and the release . . . there's nothing like it."

Leah glanced over at Joshua, who faced the front windshield with an exhibition gaze, the kind of look people get when they're seeing a piece of digital art for the first time. "So that's why you like paintings?"

"That's why everyone likes paintings," Joshua said. "Everyone can do what I do. Everyone does, all the time."

"Most of us need don't need gloves until late fall."

"Like so many other aspects of the human condition, sensitivity is a spectrum. You know that guy who looks at a Jackson Pollock and goes, 'Hell, I could do that'? He's getting nothing from the work. He's on one end. On the other side is the guy who can't look away. He feels the pull of the painting. Not what it is, but what the artist wanted it to be. If an object has been invested with emotion, people can feel it. Without touching. Like a burner on a stove. I'm wired a little different, so I grab on and get the direct induction. The full hit."

"You think I can feel things from paintings?"

"Don't you?" Joshua asked. "That's exactly what happened the first time you saw Picasso's *Boy Leading a Horse*. You weren't responding to technique and theme."

"Those things don't matter?" Leah put the black sedan on 7th.

"I don't know." Joshua tossed his hands up. "Maybe? Partly? All art is an amalgam, right? Song, player, tempo, timber, instrument, and listener. Canvas, paint, message, style, and viewer. To me, there is always another channel above those—unseen ardor. Radio waves for the soul."

"Don't go all crystals and incense on me," Leah said. "Not today."

"I won't, but—"

"Don't," Leah put her hand up between them. "I'm on the verge of accepting the fact that you may have some really super observational skills. But if you start talking about spirit guides and auras, I'm putting you back in the bullshit box."

"But—"

"Don't." Leah pushed her hand across the middle of the car.

"But—"

"I will touch you." Leah leaned to her right. On the edge of her vision she could see Joshua pushing his head against the passenger door.

"What are you, twelve?" he asked. "All I wanted to say was, all that mystical mumbo juju is all of us trying to explain what some of us feel."

"The psychics." Leah put her hand back on the steering wheel.

"Such a loaded word." Joshua returned to an upright position. "Like liberal or Muslim. The word's got too much shade."

"How about 'touched.'"

"Oh yeah," Joshua said. "That's way better."

"It's a lot to accept," Leah said. "You know?"

"Believe me, I know." Joshua drummed his fingers on the seat. They made no noise. "I would never have told you any of this if it weren't for the boy."

"Because I couldn't handle it?" Leah asked.

"That's not it."

"I'm pretty openminded," she continued.

"You are," Joshua said. "I would have preferred to ease you into it. It's tough to take all at once. Like drinking from a fire hose. My . . . attributes are better sipped than funneled."

"Yeah." Leah nodded. "This is definitely third-date stuff."

"I wouldn't know."

They stopped at a red light. Leah took the chance to look at him, still focused out over the hood and into the valleys of Manhattan. They weren't as deep in this part of town. All the brick and cornice work and billowing trees let you breathe for a moment.

"We all want something real," Joshua said. "Authenticity is just as important as the oils and canvas. If we had a machine that copied the Mona Lisa molecule for molecule, made a copy for which there would be no discernible difference between it and the original—the works would look exactly the same, feel the same, even smell the same—people would still prefer the original. You see it all the time. And by you, I mean you personally, right? People want the original and not because there is any aesthetic difference."

"You're right." Leah accelerated, moving the car onto Houston Street. "There is a premium on primes."

"If we are all just responding to light and color, that wouldn't be the case. People respond to a deeper projection from the art. From the impressions."

"I . . . a . . ." Leah had to think about it for a bit. There had to be a flaw in that argument. There also had to be better times to find it.

"Which is my long answer." Joshua broke his gaze from windshield and turned to Leah.

"I don't even remember the question." There were so many, Leah thought. They lined up deep. Angry customers in the service desk line. Who took little Stepan?' What's the deal with tonight? I'd like to return this last twenty-four hours because it doesn't fit.

"You asked me how I might help," Joshua said. "Short answer: I keep things real."

"That's not what I'm going for here," Leah said.

"It's where we're going to end up."

CHAPTER THIRTY FIVE

The Printer's Union stood as an excellent example of Romanesque Revival architecture, Leah decided. Large arched windows pro-vided the facing for the first two floors. Smaller versions of the windows served the second two, and skinny versions ran the rest of the way up. Red brick, with a restrained use of inlay and stone work. It seemed sturdy and proven. Good enough to have lasted a hundred-fifty years, and well-suited for a hundred-fifty more. The building had an inverse entrance at the corner of Houston and Lafayette, large enough to fit the stack of printing press letters, each about six feet high. A 'P' and 'U'.

"This stinks," Joshua said.

"Really?" Leah said. "You don't think that joke is—I don't know—a little nineteenth century, maybe?"

"That era is my bread and butter."

"I'm trying to cut out carbs."

Joshua snickered. "You don't look like you need to cut out any-thing."

Leah stopped before the revolving doors, spun one-eighty degrees and blocked Joshua's path. "I'm really sorry about this. I know how you feel about your personal space. But, well . . . " She took his gloved hands in hers. He laced their fingers naturally, blending them, weaving silk. She felt the tingle up through her neck. Both sides. A slight fever around her ears. Her mouth snatched a tiny cloud from the air with an audible huff. How stupifyingly lame! Did she really do that? What age did he accuse her of being back in the car? Twelve? "What are you, twelve?" he had asked. She had been much more together at twelve. Or five, or any other time in her life. She looked over her right shoulder and walked back-wards, leading Joshua into the next pie-shaped section of the revolving door. She pulled him all the way through without looking at him again. Don't look at him this close. Not less than two feet.

She broke out, twirled, held just his left hand in her right and playfully yanked him to the front desk—a large drafting table. She bounced on the balls of her feet and asked for the Events Coordinator, they had spoken on the phone earlier and she just could not wait to see the space.

They moved to the side and waited. She kept his hand in hers, and stood with her legs pressed together, ready to catch a glimpse of some boyband sneaking through the lobby.

She didn't want to like the lobby; they hammered the theme so, so, so repetitively. Floor tiles the color of egg cream. Pale pine—seasoned and shiny—edged the walls, creating blocks of pigeon-hole shelves some of which held large lead-type letters, an occasional oil can or little tool she couldn't name. A set of stools, benches and more drafting tables filled in the center of the room. Covered by low-hanging bare-bulb industrial lights. The room managed to create warmth from a factory motif. In the end, she gave in. It worked. She had to give the designers credit. The space had personality.

"What am I supposed to be?" Joshua asked. "Your boyfriend? Fiancé?"

"I hope they don't ask." She made a full smile. "Because I have no idea what you are."

A whizzing sound came from the far side of the lobby. An electric wheelchair, driven by a man in his mid-forties. Swooping black and gray hair, Buddy Holly glasses, khakis and white cotton button down. He zoomed up to them, stopped and held out his hand.

"Thad," he said. "Welcome to the Printer's Union."

Leah ran through introductions like she'd just downed a Pixie-stick macchiato and asked if they could see the party space.

Thad looked at Leah. Then Joshua. Then Leah again, face like sheet of standard, letter-size stock right out of the ream. "Sure," he said and started towards the elevator. He turned the wheelchair when they reached the doors and waited.

"You said about twenty-five guests?" Thad asked.

"You have a good memory," Leah answered.

"You did not mention a date."

"We have a couple in mind."

"Of course." The elevator doors opened. Thad backed in. Leah and Joshua followed.

"The place is amazing," Joshua said. "Lovely attention to detail."

"We have tried very hard to make it someplace special," Thad said. "For special people and special occasions."

Leah willed the elevator to climb faster. Faster! Elevators were such a waste of time. No scenery, no passers-by, nothing besides a quick chat about nothing.

The elevator opened into a small receiving area. More yellow pine and cream. Thad led them through double doors into what they called the parlor. The old print shop spirit continued, through lots of reclaimed wood and exposed brick. Tables with carriage wheels. Rolls of crisp paper standing on end. A recessed bar at the far end, with a small wooden awning. Fading manuscript pages and font charts adorned the walls. The designers had been smart and clear and stopped just short of over doing it. Leah bounded into the center and twirled. She put on her best fake smile and counted the ways into and out of the space: main entrance, one behind the bar, one more to side for staff.

"Fabulous." She stopped and beamed at Joshua. "It's going to be perfect."

"It does tend to impress." Thad smiled. "Can you tell me the dates you had in mind?" Thad asked.

"One last thing." Leah took a step toward him. "Can we see the kitchen?"

"That's not usually part of the tour," Thad said.

"If it's not too much trouble," Leah returned.

"I can assure you our kitchen will be up to your needs."

"A quick look." Leah pinched her fingers and squinted.

"They are prepping for dinner now," Thad said. "It's quite chaotic. I'm sure you can understand how disruptive a trio of intruders might be."

Leah smiled into Thad's smile.

"Leah," Joshua said. "It's OK."

"No," Leah said. "It's important. I won't be comfortable until *we* are comfortable."

"It's getting close to dinner," Joshua said. "You've seen those shows. Knives flying, pots of boiling water, people yelling 'chef!' It's probably dangerous."

"I don't know about any danger," Thad said. "But it is bustling."

"Look," Leah stated. "I don't want to be a pest, but, the fact is, we have a bit of an issue. We are not implying that your kitchen is any-thing but top notch. Not at all. We wouldn't be here if we thought otherwise. But we would feel much better if we could take a super fast peek into your kitchen." Leah held out her hands and wiggled all of her fingers. Thad watched, with a curious scowl. Leah darted her eyes at Joshua, back to Thad, and gave him the 'so sorry' look.

Thad stole a glance at Joshua's gloves and said, "I see." He turned the chair towards the double doors they had used to enter the parlor. "Maybe we can do a drive-by."

"Oh," Leah said, "Can we use the back way? We'd like to follow the exact path the catering staff would use."

Thad looked at Leah. Then Joshua. Then back at Leah.

"Sure." He turned the motorized wheelchair around again and set off across the room.

CHAPTER THIRTY SIX

Leah and Joshua stood outside the Printer's Union, facing each other. The street had become thick with people, just in the short time they'd been inside. The great change. People going home, excitement or relief overcoming their weariness. Leah had never had a job that kept a regular schedule. At the galleries, she would sometimes watch the progression through the big picture windows and consider it, the routine, the nine-to-fivers, flowing by every day. Some evenings she'd laugh at them and their dull hue routines. Other nights, she'd wonder what it might be like, having a regular schedule that put you in sync with so many others. With the majority, it always seemed, though no one she knew swam in that stream. She schooled with the late-night, skinny-dipping crowd. Until she switched sides and joined the pod that yelled at you to get out of that fountain. That pod didn't keep normal hours either.

Not normal. Never normal. Did she even know what normal might be?

"What do you think?" Joshua asked.

"I think I'm messed up." Crap, did she say that out loud?

Joshua's eyes pointed up and to the right, then darted to the left. Not a roll, as in "you're being silly." More of a thought, counter thought, with a third thought winning out.

"Are you familiar with the Sapeurs of the Congo?"

"No," Leah said. "I summer in West Egg."

"These guys dress at the height of fashion. Bespoke suits. Socks matching handkerchiefs matching ties—flamboyant and stylish, in the middle of poverty, war and death. It is very close to impossible to maintain a Savile Row wardrobe in Kinshasa, and they do it. They show off to show how society is supposed to work, regardless of mass murders, forced starvation or kidnappings."

"You're saying I'm a Sapeur?" Leah asked.

"Not even close." Joshua batted his hand. "They'd have you in a lot more color. Some color. Any color, really."

"These are my work clothes. I'm working here."

"I'm saying they figure it out," Joshua said. "They get what they can, make what they can't, and come out looking good."

"This isn't about looks."

"This is all about looks." Joshua raised his hands like he might put them on Leah's shoulders. They hovered a few inches from her. "You're running a con."

"A sting."

"A con." Joshua's hands pulsed. "The trick is getting people to look where you want, when you want, and see just what you want them to see. What's the term? *Trompe l'oeil.* To deceive the eye. That's your technique and you're very good at it."

"And you?" Leah glanced from hovering gloved hand to hovering gloved hand. "Where did you learn so much about the art of the con?"

Joshua put his hands at his sides. "Art is art. Whether you're trying to coax someone into seeing a ballerina in your slag of bronze or a moment from the Bible in layers of oil, it's all the same. Only the techniques differ. That first time we met, in the hotel with Stepan, you wanted me to see you and your FBI partner as brokers. You constructed the scene. Characters representing positions, with implied motivations, telling part of the story by way of your looks."

Leah stretched her neck, tipping her head back and around. "I'm not an artist."

"You fooled me," Joshua said.

She put her hands on her hips and sighed. "What are we going to do with Marisa?"

"We're going to worry about her later."

"I'm uncomfortable letting—"

"Then slip into something more comfortable." Joshua's lips curled again, around the corners. God, she hated that. The mischief. The misdirection. The misleading cuteness and coyness of his curly little smile. She would *not* trace her finger along his lips from whorl to whorl. Not, never, no how.

"I'm going to stay," Leah said.

"Here?" Joshua asked.

"Right here. Keep an eye on the place until we get everyone assembled."

"You think it's going somewhere? After a hundred-fifty years it's going to pack up and move to Chelsea?"

"Yes," Leah said. "That's exactly what I think. The place could pull a decent buck for this lot. It could sell out and move to Connecticut.

Would you blame it? I'm leaning that way and I've only been here thirty minutes."

Joshua looked around. "Maybe there's a decent bar around. We can watch it from the window."

"We," Leah stressed, "are going to need some cash."

His attention snapped back to her. "Oh. Yeah. Right."

"Sorry to ask. You having spent nearly a million dollars on this project already."

"Spent is not exactly the right word, but I appreciate the sentiment. How about if I run to the bank, then come back and keep you company?"

"You know I'm an FBI agent, right? This is what we do?"

"Yeah, but with partners and little things in your ears and people watching you with binoculars from a rented apartment."

"I'm not buying plutonium," Leah said. "These are art collect-ors. I've only been shot at twice by art collectors."

Joshua smiled. "I hope they didn't hit anything vital."

Leah scowled. "They never hit anything, what with their fond-ness for eighteenth century dueling pistols and all."

"Hey. I've seen *Hamilton*. They can be lethal."

"Go," Leah ordered. "Get some cash and get back here in two hours."

"Fine, fine." Joshua raised his arms again, like he might take her shoulders and lean in. He blinked. Hard. And lowered his arms. His lips moved in a similar manner. Going in for a smile, then backing out. "I'll get a cab."

"I'll see you later." Leah walked past him.

"Later, then."

She made it three paces before turning around.

Joshua waved.

Leah walked around the Printer's Union twice, making note of all the exits and entrances, whether doors had coded locks, key locks or no outside handles at all. She found the loading dock for the heavier kitchen supplies and laundry service. She located all the street- and near-street-level cameras, imagining the angle and range of each. She watched a cleaning woman, in a crisp blue and white uniform, emerge from a heavy steel door—the kind with no knob—prop it open with a mop handle and smoke. She watched two young men unfurl the garage door at the loading dock and toss out two wooden pallets. Then they watched her for a few steps. She rolled her eyes and kept walking.

Around the front, people and cars kept moving. The street was wide and extra noisy. The best spot from which to settle in and watch the entrance had been taken up by a couple of street performers. One of those living statues, painted silver across his skin and denim. A guy in fatigues and a huge knitted hat, barely holding his dreadlocks, sat next to him, slapping a small, wooden drum. She couldn't decide if the robot and the Rastafarian arrived separately and each refused to give up the space, or they worked as a duo with a fusion of theme that really, really escaped her.

She stopped in a bodega across the street, grabbed a granola bar, bottle of ginger ale, and pack of Marlboro Lights. She walked to the street across the building's back, took a spot with a good view of the service door and snacked. The big, daily migration began to fade with the light, but left plenty of people strolling back and forth, blank faces, stern walks that were hard on the heels. She knew that all too well. The City ate shoes like licorice, nibbling away at them till they were nothing.

She finished the can and the bar, opened the cigarettes and waited.

The human-sized service door opened and the cleaning woman slipped out. Leah dashed across the street, moved close to the building and approached trying to stay out of her line of sight.

As she got closer, she took out her pack of cigarettes, opened the top and tapped one out. "Could I?"

"*Sí*," the woman said.

"A light?" Leah made a lighter-flicking motion with her thumb, accompanied by a crunch of the shoulders and chagrined face.

"*Sí*," the woman took a lighter from the pouch of her apron and handed it to Leah.

"I was going to buy a lighter, but I've got, like, a bazillion at home, you know?"

"*Sí*," she said.

Don't cough, don't cough, don't cough. Leah lit up pulling the smallest drag one could make and still start the end glowing. God, when was the last time she smoked anything? Once, ten years ago?

"Ah," she said after her first puff. The nicotine buzzed her head. She handed the woman her lighter. "I keep leaving the lighters where they're not needed. Drives me crazy."

"*Sí*."

"And they're not cheap." Leah took another small drag. "I look at the little table by my front door, where I put my keys, you know?"

"*Sí*."

"I look at the table and I'm like, crap, there's got to be a hundred dollars worth of disposable lighters on that thing."

The woman sucked in the rest of her cigarette, dropped it and crushed it with the toe of her all-white sneaker.

"*Gracias*," Leah said.

"*De nada.*" The woman bent for the mop handle she'd used to keep the door open.

"Oh no," Leah darted for it. "Let me. Least I can do." She pulled it up and opened the door. The cleaning woman went through and took the mop. Leah dropped her pack as the door closed, catching it before shutting completely. "Oops. I got it."

The cleaning woman left. Leah took four cigarettes out of the pack and jammed them into the bolt well on the door jam. She pushed the door with care. The lock didn't click. She dug in with her nails and pried it open. Then she closed it again with even more care.

Breaking and entering. Unlawful access. Trespassing. She stopped listing the things with which she might charge herself, moved to the side and leaned back against the wall.

Maybe some delivery boys would walk by and she could whistle at them.

CHAPTER THIRTY SEVEN

The van pulled up at the loading dock at 7:02 PM. The van was a thirty-year-old Dodge Caravan, light blue interrupted by fake wood on the sides. Leah easily determined the fakeness of said wood because real wood did not roll up in the corners trying to escape its chrome bindings. Van drove the van. Of course. Leah shook her head. These putzes probably thought that was hysterical. Now that she thought about it, Van probably wasn't even his real name. He simply had one.

The passenger door opened and Joshua got out. Black leather shoes, indigo jeans and a black dress shirt, sleeves unbuttoned and flared showing off tight black driving gloves that very nearly looked appropriate—perfect if the vehicle had been a vintage Ferrari. Which, by a large margin, it was not.

He opened the sliding door allowing Dani, Asuna, and Scott to slide out. Scrawny penguins, in their catering garb. Leah left her spot on the corner and walked quickly to meet them in front of the human sized door next to the roll-up style door atop the dock. She looked at Joshua, who met her eyes. Dead serious. A little anxious, perhaps. She pumped her lips in the direction of a smile that never really happened, slid her nails into the metal seam of the door and yanked it open. Cigarettes were, indeed, good for something.

She took the lead, and wound her way through and up the hallways, peach colored and so skinny she couldn't believe staff carried trays through them. She found the break room where the staff congregated. Leah and Joshua ducked in. The others passed, on their way up to the parlor. As Leah and Scott entered, two young women at a small wooden table stopped talking and spun their attentions. Meerkats at the zoo.

"Hi," Leah said as if holding back a laugh. "Are you two working the party in the parlor tonight?"

The blond by bottle, mid-twenties, a hundred-ten pounds in a white blouse that had been washed a few too many times said, "A, yeah," as if it were the answer to $1 + 1$. The other, a younger woman with thick black hair and a fresh white blouse two sizes too big read them up and down. Lost guests? Hotel managers she hadn't met? Drunk idiots from some other party? Leah could tell she didn't know.

"If we could," Leah giggled into her hand. "If . . ." She laughed more and turned to Joshua, who took the third chair at the table and leaned across.

"We want to play a little prank on our friend who's throwing the party in the parlor."

"Ok . . ." the blond stretched out.

"We're wondering if you two wouldn't mind starting a little late tonight. Say 8:30."

"We're supposed to start soon," the blond said. "So says the guy who signs our checks."

"*Ohun ti o wipe?*" the woman with the black hair ask.

"*Duro, duro,*" the blond replied.

"I didn't bring my check book." Joshua took out a roll of bills and handed it to the blond.

She looked at it, looked at the other young lady and covered the money with both hands. "Is this part of the joke?"

"We appreciate your flexibility."

"We'll stay here all night, if it works for you."

"Later is good," Joshua smiled and rose. "We'll need some bacon-wrapped scallops eventually."

"Oh my God, this is going to be so funny," Leah chirped and ducked out of the room. Joshua followed.

In the hall, Leah's face went from clown to FBI agent. She couldn't stand hearing herself giggle one more millisecond. She moved quickly to the service elevator and pushed the 'up' button.

"That went well," Joshua said.

"Giving money to waitresses?" Leah said. "That didn't even make it to my list of things that might go wrong."

The elevator opened and a man in his mid-fifties got out. Black pants, white shirt—rolled up at the sleeves—small black bow-tie. The bartender, Leah hoped. They got on and hit ten.

"Still," Joshua said, "You've got admit. Everything's falling into place. You've got your people here and ready. That's pretty promising."

Leah let that hang in the air for the rest of the ride. The doors opened and they debarked into an area behind the parlor. They entered the party room, alert and ready. Scott stood behind the bar, seeming very much like the kind of hip city-dweller who knew what went into a Sazerac. Dani and Asuna hung by the side.

An empty wooden easel stood a few feet out from the center of the wall opposite the bar. Leah walked over to it. Ran her finger down the cross member, the shelf that would hold something valuable. Some-thing someone thought worth a child. Or, put another way, something overvalued by a real asshole. She walked the perimeter of the room, then exited out the staff door. She leaned back against the wall. Joshua followed her into the hall.

"Welcome to the outfield," Leah said.

"As in baseball?" Joshua asked.

"My supervisor likes to hire people who played baseball at some point in their lives. Especially fielders. People who can handle long periods of inaction followed by explosive action. He mourns the decline of baseball as America's favorite sport."

"Football can be pretty boring," Joshua said.

"It's not the same," Leah said. "Or so I've been told. In football you know when to pay attention. The guy who throws the ball actually shouts it at you. In baseball, you never know when the play's coming your way."

"I didn't take you for the sports metaphor type."

"I'm not. It's the kind of crap Dean talks about when we're sit-ting around, waiting, like now, in his proverbial outfield. And, Mr. Fawls, that's kind of sexist."

Joshua replied, "I call 'em like I see 'em. Like an umpire. The guy above the fray."

Leah gave him the slow blink.

"I'm quite used to waiting myself," Joshua said. "Without the little league training."

"Really." Leah gave her head a doubting tilt. "What do you wait for?"

Joshua's flourish of a grin returned. "Nothing now."

A cashmere blanket, wrapping around her, as light rain pattered on her windowsill. Oh man, would she rather snuggle up than everything else she was doing right now. Her stupid idea based on her stupid mistakes compounding the idiocy of the last full day. She looked at her watch. Twenty-four hours. She'd started this freakin' too-slow train wreck twenty-four hours ago. She'd been stupid before, many times, but usually not for this long.

She parted the door accessing the bar. Scott leaned forward on it.

"Anything?" she asked.

Scott turned. "The house is dead."

She closed the door and looked at Joshua. "Nobody."

"There's only a half an hour to go," he said.

"Neal should be here. Or a rep, at least, if he wanted to make a grand entrance with his mysterious item."

"A greeter would be appropriate," Joshua said. "Perhaps more than one, with this group."

Leah pressed her back against the wall. She took out her phone and checked her email. Nothing cogent. She paced around the floor, out around to the elevators—they appeared to be working—back through the hallways, checked on Dani and Asuna—meeting their deep deep scowls with her own, stood in the bar area, fought the urge to have Scott make her a drink and drifted back into the hall, where Joshua stood, leaning a shoulder to the wall, legs and arms crossed as if she had taken too long to get ready for a show and a late supper, followed by a carriage ride through the park and . . .

"This is wrong," she stated.

"What part," Joshua said. "The kidnapping, the secret auction, the con we're running?"

"They should be here," Leah said. "They, them, anyone."

"The entire invitation list consists of people who like to be fashionably late."

Leah reentered the parlor. Silence. She marched straight through to the main entrance and threw open the doors. She stared at the elevator doors. She spun and marched back into the center of the room and rammed her hands onto her hips.

"Neal," she spat.

Joshua sat on one of the tall stools. "What's the deal with Neal?"

"He moved the auction," Leah said.

"You think?"

"He didn't want us there."

"Who wouldn't? We are a very handsome couple."

"We spooked him. He's a conman."

"And you can't con a conman," Joshua said.

"Actually, you can," Leah said. "It takes a con woman."

"What does this mean?" Dani walked towards Leah. "They're not coming?"

Leah saw herself in the young woman. Every emotion cracking open on Dani's face marked her own. Anger. Bewilderment. Anguish. Dani had a double scoop of that last one. The denial of redemption meant you failed at doing good while the bad remained on your permanent record.

"God damn it!" Dani's fists balled and bounced in the air. "Do you know what we did to get here right now? What we all gave up? The favors, the lies, the money—all so we could help that little boy and now you're saying you got it wrong? You fucked it up? You, the super special agent in the fucking God damned FBI!"

The air whistled out of Leah. She felt the prick to her lame-ass balloon figure. "Hey, little girl," the man had said, "What can I make you?" Leah replied, "An FBI agent." Squeak, squeak, done, pretend. Then Dani. Then the stab. Now Leah's arms and legs and little blue egghead sagged and wrinkled and soon she'd flop on the floor, waiting for the broom and pan.

The staff door crashed open. Boris leapt in, a belt of bombs in full view, red wires leading to his right hand and a detonator switch.

"Nobody should move!"

CHAPTER THIRTY EIGHT

"Have a seat," Joshua said to Boris. "Change of plans."

Boris looked around. Leah was impressed that he didn't let his puzzlement—and there had to be a ton of it—show.

"By 'change of plans'," Scott said from the bar, "he means we've gone from *having* plans to yelling at each other in an empty bar. Can I get you anything?"

Boris stood, eyes fixed on Leah.

Leah took out her phone and called Oscar Pierce. It rang six times, went to voice mail, and she gave up.

"Who else do we know?" she half-shouted to Joshua.

Joshua already had his phone up to his ear. "Stepan," he said and paused. "Did you receive any word that the auction had moved tonight? . . . No? . . ."

"No?" Leah snapped. "That doesn't make any sense."

"Because I'm here," Joshua continued into the phone. "They didn't say anything about me not coming tonight."

"This is so wrong." Leah paced in a small circle.

"Come on up," Joshua said. "The kidnapper is not here."

"Mr. Markov is coming up?" Boris asked.

"I'm afraid so."

Boris turned to Scott and said, "Vodka."

Scott poured him a shot

"You should think about the back door," Joshua said to Boris. "I have no idea how he might see this."

Boris stood like a concrete pylon, his eyes fixed on Leah. She looked back long enough for him to know she had both a good hour's worth of things to tell him . . . and nothing. She nodded once.

He raised his glass and said, "We all die." He threw back the shot and exited through the staff door.

"Who is Mr. Markov?" Dani asked.

"The little boy's father," Leah answered.

Dani looked like she might throw up.

"Go downstairs to Van and the van and wait for us," Leah said in a soft voice. She raised her head so Asuna and Scott could hear. "All of you."

They looked at each other. Leah realized they were quite good at communicating without words. A good team. A good troupe. They slipped out through the staff door.

Leah checked her watch. 8:05. The auction had started some-where. She had lost and now she'd get to tell Stepan Markov about it in person. Then, tomorrow, she'd get to tell Dean about all the emails, draining the tank on the sedan, and simply not showing up for work. She would be called an amateur. Recommended for disciplinary action or worse. She knew this, because that is what she would do if some junior agent pulled this garbage on her. Either way, the trust would be lost.

Dean's trust in her judgment. She knew that, too, because she had none left. He'd catch up to her. Or was it down?

She had it once, Dean's trust. And she needed it because she had none of her own at the time. She had recently become The Turner Girl, and this moment reminded her so much of that one, she wanted to faint. Why didn't women faint anymore? She totally got why it used to be so common. Come on, seriously, there are times when placing the back of your wrist to your forehead and flopping to the floor is a highly attractive solution to your ills. Sure, it sets the woman's movement back two hundred years, but was she leading the cause? Couldn't we have, like, one little setback now and then, as in right now, not then? If women really were strong they'd recover from her having a little spell, sinking to the hardwood and feigning unconsciousness until Stepan came and left.

The Turner Girl. She fought so hard to escape that nickname. Maybe the nickname was all she really escaped. That wide-eyed, over-ambitious, sucker of a girl still drove things from deep inside her. She'd never really get away. You can't escape the prison if you are the prison.

I'm not letting him get away, Leah swore to herself as Archie eyed the door, three years ago, in the middle of The Wen gallery.

"You brought something?" Leah motioned to the large portfolio hand-cuffed to Archie's wrist.

"A little something," he replied. "I thought Bat might be interested." Bat. Archie had used the owner's nickname. Only his inner-most circle called him Bat. "It appears he's not with us today."

"Somewhere over the Pacific," Leah said. "Why don't you give me a look?"

Archie stood with knees slightly bent, arms slightly raised, eyes dashing back and forth between Leah and the door. An internal argument played out Kabuki style. Slow, measured, full of meaning. And total theatre, Leah would later learn. The hard way.

I'm not letting him get away, she repeated in her head. "A little peek couldn't hurt," she said out loud.

Archie smirked. "Do you have somewhere more private?"

"Certainly." Leah led Archie to the back office.

She rounded her small white desk. Archie fiddled with a small key, unlocked the cuffs, and unzipped the leather case. He drew out a nine-by-twelve canvas, unframed. Leah needed less than a second to declare it beautiful. The sun setting over a river, running through the middle of a city . . . Victorian. London. Smoke and haze and hues of deep umber, ochre and gold. The reflection of the sun swirled and darkened, as if something lurked just under the surface and used the sunlight as a disguise. Gorgeous, enriching . . .

"A Turner," slipped from her mouth.

"One of his later works," Archie said. "One of his best, if you ask me."

She let the painting wash over her. An original Joseph Mallord William Turner rested on her desk. It had to be worth millions. So many millions, it could not be here. It could not be real.

"I'm not familiar with the work," she said in an unsteady voice.

"Don't feel ashamed," Archie said. "Not too many are. He gifted it to a family, who hid it during the Blitz. It was only uncovered a few years ago, so it has escaped the most recent catalogue raisonné."

"It is . . . stirring."

"It's the cow urine," Archie said.

"I'm sorry," she had said. "It sounded like you said cow urine."

"Turner had a man who fed his cows nothing but mangos," Archie continued. "He collected the urine for Turner, who used it in his paint to get those breathy, natural yellows. They're unmistakable, aren't they?"

"It is a beautiful piece," Leah said.

Archie smiled a knowing, worldly smile. They were in on a secret, the two of them. They could appreciate a painting like few others.

"No offense," he said. "But I'd hoped Bat would be here. I thought he might be interested."

"He would be if it were for sale."

"Sadly," Archie said, "it is very much is for sale."

"He'll be back next week," Leah said.

"Alas and alack, I will be elsewhere." He laughed. "Can't remember where at the moment. Madrid, I think. Or Mauritania. Something that begins with an 'M'."

"I'm sure he will be interested."

"Oh, don't tell him I was here," Archie said. "It will break his heart to know he missed out."

"You have another buyer," Leah said.

"No, but I will. The owner needs to dispose of the asset quickly." Archie leaned over the desk to whisper, despite no one within ear or eyeshot. "The most miserable of the Three Ds, I'm afraid. Divorce. The owner needs to liquidate the asset and hide the revenues. No time or taste for a proper auction."

"A couple of days," Leah said.

"Oh dear," Archie said. "Now I'm breaking your heart. Absolutely the last thing I'd ever want to do. I am in quite a hurry, though. I was sent to make a deal this afternoon and it collapsed. I stopped in to see Bat because he's a friend and because I don't care to repatriate the painting. There is another buyer on the Continent. How could there not be, right? But the dower glares of Customs once more . . . well, I can think of better ways to spend my time."

He's not getting away, Leah said again, in her head. This kind of deal could vault a career up and over years of work and waiting and wanting. If Bat wasn't on a plane, if she just had another handful of hours, she could make this work.

"When are you leaving the city?" Leah asked.

"Tonight," Archie replied. "A redeye to London."

"Why don't you let us ship it for you? You're not going to need it tomorrow are you? Or even Sunday, for that matter."

"That is a kind offer," Archie said. "But I really can't just leave it here."

"I will write you a receipt."

Archie smiled. "Please, again, don't take offense. Your offer is very sweet. But I'm a foreign national and I don't actually own the painting myself. It's owned by a company with an address in Cypress. It is very convoluted. Only a bill-of-sale would hold any water across the pond."

Leah didn't understand the details. She'd never done a deal like this. Still, she would not display any signs of ignorance.

"What we really need is some collateral," Archie said.

"I can't very well send you off with another painting," Leah said. "It defeats the purpose."

"Mmmm." Archie played with his chin.

"I'll make a deposit," Leah said. "And we'll write the paper work up that way."

"What way?"

"As a deposit on a sale. It will let you negotiate the final sale price with Bat when he's back on the ground. If that doesn't work, we ship. You either make a sale or avoid traipsing around Manhattan with couple million dollars-worth of art cuffed to your wrist."

Archie tipped his head way back and rubbed his chin more. He let out a large sigh, lowered his head and said, "Lovely. Let's do it."

"I'm only authorized to wire $250,000," Leah said.

"That's fine. It's just a deposit. I trust you."

That last line knocked around in her head all the time. She could still hear it with perfect clarity. She could still see Archibald Lee smile widely as he said it. The image stayed fresh because it was the final one. No images of Archie came after it.

If she hadn't been twenty-seven, late on a Friday afternoon, with her boss in an airplane—the only time he could not be reached—and so damn anxious to make an impact. If she had not wanted so badly to be the cat who drops that mouse on the stoop. The little girl who made people smile at the gallery with her delightful insight into an abstract expressionism. If, if, if . . .

She wouldn't be here now, wanting to punch herself in the gut she'd trusted again.

The elevator doors swooshed open. Out stepped a Rastafarian and a living statue.

CHAPTER THIRTY NINE

Leah thought about pulling her gun. On instinct. The Rastafarian and the big guy in silver body paint—with matching silver overalls—looked so wrong, they had to be trouble. They were marching, not ambling. Aimed, with purpose and direction. They weren't lost. They weren't just checking things out.

As they entered, the gleaming statue took a position at the door. A fake robot bodyguard. Arms straight down, like pipes on the sides of a semi. The Rastafarian dude grabbed the edge of his plump, stripped, stocking hat and tugged it off, flinging it Frisbee-style without a care as to where it flew. He had a nice head of golden hair. It failed to match his olive military jacket, faded T-shirt and jeans last washed in a jet engine. Leah could see the face now. Stepan Markov. She looked back at the silver guy and squinted. She made out Yuri's face under the metallic makeup.

Stepan walked towards Joshua like he might not stop. Like he might plow him through the café tables and chairs and into the wall. "What are you doing here?" he demanded.

"Our best." Joshua didn't move.

"And you, Special Agent Capello? Can you have a reason for being here?" His accent came through. He didn't have complete control of himself. Never a good thing.

"We thought we could help," she said.

"Even after I said I did not want your help."

"I think we both want to the same thing," Leah said.

"Oh?" Stepan snapped. "Did we both want you fucking things up? I do not remember that. Do you remember that, Joshua?" Stepan stopped in the middle of the room, three feet from his friend. "Do you remember me saying please go and fuck up this deal and put my son in more danger?"

Joshua dipped his head to the right. Just a few degrees. Just enough to show a little weariness with Stepan's sarcasm. "Remember when he was born, Stepan? I flew to Moscow to see him. Lidiya brought him out all swaddled and cooing in that cloud of a blanket. Such a beautiful child. Radiant. You took him and went to hand him to me. 'My most precious work of art,' you said. And you tried to hand him to me, and . . ."

The two men looked at each other, mouths locked tight, shrink wrapped in skin. Leah knew better than to say a word. She stood watching. Like Yuri. Like a bodyguard. Paying devout attention, under-standing when the best action is inaction.

Understanding the flipside, too. She was not Yuri or Boris or that chick at Oscar Pierce's place. She was not a bodyguard at all. She was an agent of the . . .

That chick at Pierce's place. Vita. She knew all kinds of things.

Leah pinched the lapel of her black jacket and slowly spread it open. "Taking out my phone, Yuri. Don't mess your makeup."

He didn't budge or ripple. He'd gone back to being a statue. He was quite good at it.

"What happened to the auction?" Stepan asked Joshua.

"We think the seller, or seller's agent, moved the location at the last minute," Joshua answered.

Leah found Vita's text from earlier in the day. She typed, "Where is the auction now?" and hit send.

"Moving a sale like this is not good," Stepan said.

"I think it's going to feature one piece." Joshua pointed a leather-clad thumb back at the empty easel. "One piece shouldn't be too difficult to move."

"The buyers," Stepan said. "We are not easy to move. I do not know the other people invited, but I know I planned to be here several months ago. I would not be happy to have it changed."

"Several months ago?" Leah asked.

"Around Christmas," Stepan answered.

Leah said, "Huh," and brought her phone back up. She sent Vita another message. "NOW!"

"If this were my deal, I would keep it close," Stepan continued. "I would not want to piss off my buyers."

"No," Joshua nodded. "I agree. You want them in a buying mood. A dash of mystery is nice. Too much and the whole thing looks fishy."

"Which is why I would have brought you along."

"And here I am. Funny, huh?"

"No," Stepan said. "Nothing about this is funny."

"Not funny, like a joke," Joshua said. "You know. Weird."

"I don't know weird." Stepan turned to Leah. "So you have no idea where the auction has moved."

"None," Leah returned. Her phone vibrated in her hand. The message from Vita said, 'Why?'

Leah wanted to tell her that she was in the mood to buy some art. She had ten million dollars in the bank and blank wall in her boudoir and both just had to go. Instead, she typed "U know Y" and pressed send.

She had no idea what Vita knew, but she wasn't ignoring Leah's texts. She must be a real pro. She must sense something's not right and therefore willing to trade her info for a chance at more.

Joshua said to Stepan, "What surprises me is that you don't know the new auction site either. Why wouldn't they tell you about the change? You're on the invite list. You're a dependable collector with plenty of cash."

"Someone has gone through very much trouble to keep me out of this buy."

"Yes . . ." Joshua rubbed his chin. "But that was the kidnapper. Not the people putting on the auction."

"Unless they are one in the same," Stepan snarled.

"But then why kidnap your son?" Joshua said. "If they didn't want you there, they could've simply not invited you."

Stepan clasped his hands behind his head and stretched his arms. He grunted through grinding teeth and took a few steps in a very small circle.

Leah's phone jiggled again. Another message from Vita. It read, "Brozilla."

Yep, Leah chirped in her head. Brozilla made a cruel kind of sense. The biker bar used as a rehearsal space by the Boss Level Crea-tures. The place they'd held a gun on her, just last night. *Yep, yep, flippity freakin' yep.*

She had to ditch the billionaire Rasta and his Tin Man.

CHAPTER FORTY

Leah did not want Stepan and Yuri following her to Brozilla. They were both ready to pull triggers and drop bodies. She could tell. In this state of mind, in defense of his four-year-old, Stepan could justify any action. She didn't blame him, nor did she need him. Leah could get the little boy back without loading up an emergency room, filling out reports and losing her job.

Right? She could totally do this. Go Leah!

Except Leah wanted Joshua with her at Brozilla. He came in handy. She didn't fully understand the mechanisms, but he had a gift for gleaning information. And that was absolutely the reason she wanted to bring him along. Straight up. Intelligence gathering. She needed him for that and no other reason. All she had to do was separate Joshua from Stepan and Yuri, and slip away without being noticed.

Tough to do when you're the only four people in the room.

Brozilla sat fifteen minutes away. Less than ten with use of lights and the siren. If the auction still started at eight, she was screwed. If Neal needed a bit of extra time per the change of venue, she was slightly less than screwed. She'd been to auctions. People took their time. Especially with millions of dollars on the line, and Leah knew Neal Pozner hadn't put together this show, with that list of players, to liquidate a print from a new find in SoHo. This deal would be a big deal.

You can do this, she said to herself. Calm down. *You've got, like, eight seconds to spare.*

Stepan and Joshua grumbled away about Milan and a possibly similar circumstance, which she couldn't believe and wanted to hear all about, but couldn't. She needed to concentrate. She thumbed Scott's phone number on her phone and brought up the texting screen. She typed, "need distraction" and pressed send. She added, "don't get shot."

"Because of a bad ham," Joshua said.

"That is a much different reason for moving an auction," Stepan returned.

"I'm just saying, these things happen. I think everything is going to be fine."

"Then why are you here?" Stepan sneered from the center of his mouth. "You don't care about money, so the only reason you would go against my wishes is if you thought you could help. If everything is going to be fine, then little Styopa does not need your help. No?"

"No," Joshua defended. "Helping is not always about need."

"You want to be the hero? Is that the thing? You are helping you? Maybe you want to show off for your *ljubimaja*?"

"He is not much of a show off." Leah stepped forward, forcing the two men to form a circle near the center of the parlor. "In fact, he tries to keep all of his best tricks a secret. Mr. Markov, I can't imagine how you are feeling, but Joshua's not part of the problem. He's trying to be part of the solution. We've both been scrambling around for the past twenty-five hours hoping to uncover something. Anything that might help."

"I did not ask for your help," Stepan spat. "I clearly said no to it."

"Are you familiar with Aubrey Beardsley?" Leah asked.

"Should I be?" Stepan asked back.

"He's best known for illustrating Oscar Wilde's play *Salome*. Anyway, just as he was gaining fame, he got sick. He knew he was dying so he told his publisher to destroy all of his most recent drawings. They were slightly erotic. He wanted them burned upon his death. A wish his publisher fully ignored. Those drawings are each worth about a quarter of a million dollars today."

"What is your point?" Stepan demanded. "That people do not get what they want? Because I do."

"My point is, Beardsley didn't have all the facts," Leah returned. "He didn't know how tastes would change, people would become more permissive of such art."

A noise behind her. Joshua and Stepan glanced over her right shoulder. She followed their lines of sight and found Scott setting up behind the bar, not paying them any attention. The door to the side of the bar opened. Asuna and Dani emerged with silver trays.

Leah turned back to Stepan. "Beardsley didn't know that one day his rather risqué drawings would not be considered trashy, but just the opposite. One can be immensely talented and still not know every-thing."

Asuna appeared on Leah's left, offering a spread of stuffed mushroom caps. Dani appear on Leah's right, with cantaloupe wrapped in prosciutto. Leah and Joshua politely declined. Stepan waved them off.

"Doesn't that go both ways?" Stepan said to Leah. "Maybe there are things you don't know."

"Ha," Leah blurted with no mirth. "You can't imagine how much I don't know."

"AAAAGGGGG!" came from Dani. The tray crashed to the wood floor, spinning and bouncing light.

"What?" Asuna shouted.

Dani held clenched hands near her gaping mouth. "It moved!" She pointed at Yuri. Yuri shrugged.

"Son of a bitch!" Asuna raised her tray like a shield, dumping two pounds of mushrooms near the field of melon chunks. She cowered behind it. "Did you see that?"

Leah grabbed Joshua's forearm.

Stepan glared at the waitresses. "It's a man!"

"What's going on?" Scott ran towards them.

Leah tugged Joshua backwards a step.

Yuri raised his arms. The girls screamed. Leah could see Yuri's dumbfounded look through the layers of silver.

"It's nothing," Stepan said. "It's just a man."

"It's supposed to be art!" Dani wailed as she ducked behind Scott and Stepan.

"Son of a bitch!" Asuna said again.

"It's makeup!" Stepan yelled.

"Then why doesn't it talk?" Scott stooped and picked up a tray.

"He can talk," Stepan said.

Scott moved in front, holding the silver serving tray like it might offer some kind of protection.

"I knew this place was haunted!" Dani shouted.

"I should've listened to you," Asuna shouted back.

"Look to the light!" Scott shouted. "Your time here has passed!"

Leah tugged Joshua again. They took two more steps towards the back of the room.

"We've got make a break for it," Scott ordered. "Out that door!"

"You are nuts," Stepan twisted to move in front of Scott.

Scott spun. Dani ducked. Asuna screamed again. Stepan slipped on the mushroom—cantaloupe slick and Dani made sure he went down.

Leah didn't see anything after that. She and Joshua ran through the back hall.

CHAPTER FORTY ONE

Leah had never used the lights and sirens. Ever. Even in training she didn't bother. The flashing and noise were exhilarating, in a little-boy kind of way, but they were not conducive to streamlined though—along with Joshua, the improv troupe and everything else that just happened. Driving fast through Manhattan, though—that cleared the senses.

New Yorkers are famous for the ease with which they raise their middle fingers. They are, by legend, prickly, hurried and angry at the imposition you pose before you've even posed it. Just last week Leah had been told to get moving. She was in line at a coffee shop. Third in line. The gruff legend persists because New Yorkers like it. Being known as tough and formidable has its uses. It is, however, a legend. When you live within twelve inches of eighteen other people, there has to be a good portion of give with your take. Leah saw a bit of that now. Cars parting, bikes stopping, people holding back from walkways, because the lights and sirens said she might be on her way to help someone.

She turned the flashy racket off a good block from Brozilla. Joshua hadn't said a word the whole ride, which, she glanced at her watch, had taken nine minutes. She nosed the car up on the sidewalk near a line of five motorcycles. She panned the street with hard-fought care. Her body had no patience for methodical anything. Go, go, go—her brain battled her body and won. She surveyed the block.

A black town car at the corner. Diplomatic plates. The butt of a large, black SUV stuck out from the next cross street, taillights glowing red. A lovely turquoise Porsche two spaces back, in a loading zone. None of these vehicles were unusual for the City. For this street? Either someone was shooting a realty show or she'd found the auction. And at least a few of the attendees were still in attendance.

She wanted to do a complete walk-around. They didn't have the time. Once this party split, so did her line to the child.

Leah leaned forward on the seat and pulled out her pistol. She checked the chamber and clip. She returned it to the holster and sat.

She should call for backup. She'd found a crime in progress. She'd found the actual criminal, if she guessed right. This would be the time to summon the troops, storm the fort and insure nothing else went wrong, that no one got away, that the little boy would get home soon, in his own bed, with his loving mom and dad.

The storm. They could hit with such force that everything got blown away, washed out in the breach—busted, broken, bye-bye. Bye-bye.

"What are you doing?" Joshua asked in a soft voice.

They looked at the black door of the biker's club. Black trim, black bricks, black hardware. So meticulously menacing it ruined its own effect. It doth, Leah decided, protest too much.

"Catching my breath. And not because you took it away," Leah said. "If that's what you thought."

"Ah . . . no?" Joshua's eyes darted around.

"Good," she said. "Let's check out some art."

She flipped the door handle and jumped out of the car.

She pushed into the club. Narrow as a coffin. Weak white lights throwing down just enough glow for the bartender to tell his ryes from his bourbons. Two tons of fun sat at the bar, looking highly similar to boys who sat there the previous night. Lots of leather and chains. Lots. The bartender hadn't changed. In fact, it looked as though he hadn't changed anything. He still wore a leather vest that made him look like he'd shrunk.

The bikers watched Joshua. The bartender addressed Leah.

"Sorry," he said. "Private party tonight."

Leah walked up to the bar. She could feel Joshua a step behind her. "That's why we're here. Upstairs or down?"

"Hey," he said. "You two were in here last night."

"We'll reminisce later. Which way?"

"I don't think you're on the guest list."

Leah backed away and started towards the deep, black hall in the back. "I would've been thankful if you could've saved me a step."

"I know you're not on the list," the bartender protested.

Joshua smiled. "She's had it with lists." He followed her.

She remembered that the downstairs had been chopped up into smaller rooms. Scott said the Boss Level Creatures rehearsed here—which seemed hard to do in those little nests—so maybe the upstairs had an open layout. They climbed the flight and stopped. The top of the stairs ended with a black wooden door. No hall or platform. She twisted the black knob and pushed in.

The room was wide and plain. The center glowed white, creating so much contrast everything outside couldn't be seen. The glow came from four work-lights on tripods. The kind you'd see a road crew using at three in the morning. They formed a lit space within the dark space. In the center of that light stood an easel. On that easel leaned a large piece of golden parchment with a deep, detailed sketch in reddish umber. A man, every muscle detailed and shaded, holding a woman bent back. Swooning.

People stood around. She failed to count. The art fixated her. The line work, the media, the bold definition—she knew the piece: A recently discovered drawing by Michelangelo di Lodovico Buonarroti Simoni.

Dubbed the *Lockport Sketch*, everyone in the room probably knew this drawing. It had generated quite a bit of news a few years ago, as a re-discovery at a home in upstate New York. It had supposedly been in the family for generations, brought over from the old country, and hung in a succession of living rooms since such things came into fashion. No one ever considered the potential value.

Then, if Leah remembered correctly, the last of the parents passed and the kids had the modest estate evaluated. The estimator came to the home, expecting a bunch of worn-out post-war furniture, walked into the living room, looked up at the wall and fainted. After being revived, she asked where that drawing had come from.

None of the kids knew for sure. Before coming to America, the history of the sketch could best be described as sketchy.

Art experts don't like sketchy. They hate to hear 'huh' and see shoulders shrug. What they want, always, is an unbroken line. In this case, from 1920 back to 1520. With many great works of art, that can actually be done. Not with this sketch. Lacking clear provenance, art experts around the world asked for a series of tests. The family balked. Some of the tests—paper and ink verification—required samples that would be destroyed in the process. Some seemed like a waste—DNA tests could not be conclusive. A few made the cut, multispectral imaging mostly, that could put the paper and the ink in the right era.

Most scholars believed the sketch to be an original Michelangelo. Most everyone wanted that to be the case. Leah had not heard much after that. She assumed the big galleries were putting on their best dog and Prada shows to woo the owners.

She never expected to see greatest art-find of the last decade in a biker bar, with a sale handled by a guy who couldn't get into a preview night if he was carting crates.

"It can't be," Joshua said with next to no air.

"It explains the craziness," Leah returned. "Let's get a better—"

Steel pressed to the back of her head.

"Let's not," came a voice without a bottom.

"Great," Leah said. "Another freakin' gun to my head."

"It is a disturbing trend," Joshua said.

Leah felt the cold steel leave her skull.

"Hands behind your heads," came the voice. "Slowly."

"You know when people say 'if I had a gun to my head?'" Leah asked. "I have a baseline line now. I can answer that question and not be all hypothetical."

"We are getting to be accomplished targets, aren't we?" Joshua replied.

"And quietly," the voice said. "I should've said that."

Leah laced her fingers under her ponytail and peered into the circle of light. No one in the party seemed to have noticed the new guests. The tail of her jacket flipped up and the weight of her sidearm vanished. She felt a hand brush down the inside of her left leg. She considered a mule kick. She could guess the whereabouts of the man's head. She could also guess as to the direction of a stray bullet if the guy was twitchy. Into Joshua's torso. She let him check her right leg. In absence of any more touching or commands, she guessed he checked Joshua for weapons as well.

"Walk on," the man said. "I'll tell you all when to stop."

Leah moved her right elbow back an inch to glance at Joshua. He did the same and smiled. They faced the light and walked in step. The clatter of three people on painted hard wood caught someone's attention. The resulting pause in the party-chatter spread across the small crowd. Like when Cinderella makes her entrance, Leah thought. Kind of like that. A little.

Neal Pozner held the center of the room, an arm's length from the sketch. He held a tall, half-filled champagne flute and an expression Leah very much enjoyed. A stunned smile. Leah didn't linger on it. She panned left to right. A woman of Asian descent, five-three, thin as a lily, in an ivory suit. She couldn't guess her age but felt comfortable identifying her as Li Lau. Next to her stood Marcella Alvaro, whom she knew by sight. Or by the Vera Wang cocktail dress, gold with more beads than a craft fair. A pale, fit man in a black suit looked at Leah over his shoulder. Six-foot, mid-sixties, trying his best to stay under two-hundred pounds. He looked puzzled through his tight reddish beard, squinting through the light, checking her out, more than assessing a possible threat. Pig. He might have been Rohan Kavanagh but she decided on Piggy for the time being.

"Can I put my arms down now?" she asked.

"Keep walking," came the bass track.

Oscar Pierce drank champagne on the right side of the circle, next to another portly man, in a well-fit black suit. His black silk shirt had pleats, with pearl studs up to the collar. No tie. No sense hiding pearls like those, Leah figured. Lac Khor, she went on figuring.

Finally, she said to herself. Everyone in one place.

"My lucky night," she said out loud as they entered the ring of light.

"Lucky you weren't shot," Neal said. "I'm so sorry for the exuberant security, but as you can see—" He motioned to the sketch with both arms, as a magician's assistant might. "I need to take security quite seriously."

"We're not here for a heist," Leah said.

"Anymore," Joshua said. Leah gave him The Glance.

"Certainly not," Neal returned. "Oh, please put your arms down."

Leah straightened her jacket. Joshua raised his arms farther, stretching. Then he dropped them to his sides.

"Patrick," Neal aimed at the man behind Leah. "This is Special Agent Leah Capello of the FBI. I'm not so concerned about her, al-though I do question her taste in men." Neal stepped in front of Joshua and took a short sip of his drink. "Fawls, here, is an international art thief and conman. Exactly the kind of person I wanted to keep out of this soirée."

The others murmured, glanced at themselves. Leah could feel the uneasiness growing. The space had an off-off-off Broadway feel that not one of them would find quaint. They'd been moved here at the last minute. Now, there were guns and criminal allegations. Neal couldn't hold this group together much longer.

"What's going on here, Neal?" Piggy asked.

"Drama," Neal drawled. "It wouldn't be an auction without it, right?"

"I don't come for the drama." Piggy looked at Leah and winked.

She wanted her gun back. No, really, she needed her sidearm. She turned around and six-two, two-forty pound, white male in his mid-thirties. A blondish beard big enough to hide a slice of double-cheese with pepperoni and a gut she couldn't punch through. It had to be deeper than her arm was long. He wore a black jacket and pants, with a white T-shirt. A biker in his funeral suit. And a revolver in his right hand, dull metallic, politely pointed at the floor.

She opened her mouth, when Neal said, "Please escort Mr. Fawls out."

"Wait," Leah blurted. "I'd prefer that he stay."

"You don't get to make that call," Neal said. "I shouldn't need to remind you that you're not on the guest list either."

"He's working with me."

"Really?" Neal cocked his head to the right. "Do you work with a lot of art thieves?"

"He's not a thief."

"Did you inquire as to the origins of that Francis Bacon he passed to me this morning? Did you check out your FBI database as any proficient FBI agent would?"

Leah looked at Joshua. His wide eyes circled hers, refusing to meet them.

"He can be very charming. That's how con men work."

"He charmed you, once," Leah said. "At Art Basel Hong Kong."

"Yes." Neal turned his back to Joshua and flickered his empty hand. "Get him out of here."

"Let's get started please." Li Lau stared straight at the art. She appeared to have no interest in anything else.

"Yes, let's." Oscar Pierce gave Leah a sturdy frown.

"I'll be outside," Joshua said. Patrick pointed back towards the door with his gun.

"Art Basel was this past March," Leah said.

Neal didn't look at her as he stationed himself again next to the sketch.

Leah slid next to Piggy. "And you received your invite when? January?"

"Something like that," Piggy said. "Around the first of the year."

"So, what's a girl go to do to get a drink around here?"

Piggy grinned, the squint lines flashing back from his cresting. The unusual lighting made them extra deep. "Allow me." Piggy crossed in front of her. Two steps later, he bent over a yellow Yeti cooler, over-flowing with ice. The green necks of champagne bottles protruded. A few glasses sat on small folding stool next to it. Leah skipped up behind him.

"Ladies and gentlemen," Neal announced. "Sorry for the delay. Now, where was I before that exciting interruption?"

Piggy handed Leah a tall, fluted crystal glass. She pinched it by the stem.

"You are all familiar with the *Lockport*," Neal continued. "It's been authenticated through several sources and should be at the Chris-tie's or Sotheby's Spring events, but the owners decided on a much more direct route to the only buyers that really mattered. They wished things done quickly and without pageantry, so here we are, with the only new work from Michelangelo in four-hundred years."

A strange fog of hisses, shallow gasps and guttural sounds spread through the circle of light and out into the donut of darkness. Piggy presented a bottle, ready to pour into Leah's glass. She snapped her glass against the mouth of the bottle, shattering the top half. She shook the glass as she maneuvered herself next to the sketch.

She held the glimmering crystal teeth less than an inch from the center of the parchment and shouted, "Nobody move or the drawing gets it!"

CHAPTER FORTY TWO

As Leah expected, nobody moved. This group would collapse at the sound of her tearing through a Michelangelo. She spun the broken glass in her hand so the nasty end came from the pinky-side of her balled-up fist. Maximum cutting power, even if the bend of her arm made for an awkward stance. While the massive inhales of those gathered drifted back out of everyone's lungs she made a quick scan of the room. All the bidders stood in the ring of light. Outside the ring, the blackness became impenetrable. She'd lost track of Joshua and the door-biker with the gun. Patrick, Neal called him.

"Agent Capello, please," Neal said in a calm voice.

"Joshua? Patrick?" she yelled into the dark. "You can come on back now."

"What is your problem?" Oscar Pierce stepped forward. "You've been screwing with this shindig all day."

"Call them back, Neal," Leah commanded.

"As soon as you put the glass down," he replied.

"My question was not rhetorical," Oscar said. "What's your fucking problem?"

"I will tell you in one sec," Leah said. "Neal, where's the boy?"

He looked astonished. "What are you talking about?"

"Stepan Markov Jr. You have him and I want him back."

"This in insane," Neal said.

"Kidnapping?" Oscar scoffed. "Kidnapping a Markov?"

A cold prickle ran through the group. Leah could hear the effect on their various vocal chords. The silence became pure. No rumbles. No breathing. No steps near the door.

"It didn't make much sense to me, either," Leah said. "But Neal had no choice. At first, I thought someone here didn't want Stepan Sr. attending this auction. They didn't want to bid against him. But nobody knew the list of attendees. Only Neal."

"That makes even less sense," Neal said. "Why invite Markov in the first place, if I didn't want him to come?"

"Because it wasn't Markov you wanted to keep from attending." Leah's arm shook a little. She couldn't hold this position for long. "You didn't want Markov's appraiser here. You couldn't afford to have Joshua Fawls at your event."

"Ah," Oscar nodded.

"That makes even less sense," Neal snapped. "Put the glass down!"

Oscar said, "Neal couldn't tell Markov to leave Joshua home. Then he'd know there was a problem with the sketch. Markov might have shown up and told everyone, just for sport."

"Where's the boy, Neal?" Leah asked with acid.

"There is something wrong with you," Neal returned. "I think Fawls is clouding your judgment. He does that, you know."

"This has nothing to do with him," Leah said. "It has to do with you. And this place. You saw a woman perform here. Then you used that same woman in your kidnapping crew. It's all connected."

"Like I'm some kind of criminal mastermind?" Neal put his back to Leah and threw his arms wide. "I am so sorry everyone. We will be done with nonsense momentarily."

"Why isn't Markov here?" Li Lau had a viola for a voice. It penetrated the room not with volume, but with tone. "He is the biggest buyer for this sort of thing."

"You'd have to ask Markov," Neal said.

"Call your man back," Leah said. "He lacks direction."

Oscar crossed his arms. "If this drawing were an original Michelangelo, Neal wouldn't care who Markov brought to verify authenticity."

"The drawing's an original," Neal stated. "The tests were un-questionable."

Marcella Alvaro spun on the points of her shoes and began her click, click, click to the door.

"Mrs. Alvaro," Neal said. "Please."

The circle closed in.

Li Lau looked at Oscar. "The friend of Markov is an expert on Michelangelo?"

"No," Oscar replied. "He has a gift for identifying fakes. Markov won't buy a poster from the MoMA shop without him."

"He came with this woman?" Li Lau ran Leah up and down.

"It's all very strange," Oscar said.

"Too strange." Lac Khor backed out of the light. The last thing Leah saw of him were four pearls dotting the darkness.

"Mr. Khor," Neal pleaded. "The auction will start—"

"Now." Piggy stepped into Leah's viewing area, on her left. He fixed his eyes on the sketch. "I'll give you $900,000 for it. Right now. No more questions."

"You think it's real?" Oscar asked.

"I just said I'd pay $900,000 didn't I?" Piggy returned.

Oscar offered a million.

"The sketch is not for sale." Leah waggled the broken champagne flute, smattering light.

"Stop that!" Neal held back a full yell.

"I want the boy," Leah snarled back. "Now!"

"If it's real," Piggy started, "it's worth considerably more than a million."

"If it is real," Lia Lau added. "That is the question. I don't know about a boy or kidnapping. I know if the painting is real, the story is silly." She took in a little extra air and said just shy of a shout, "Patrick! Bring Markov's friend here now."

She faced Neal. Leah wished she could see his face. She wanted to see the kind of expression he chose to meet that look. Li Lau's express-ion was flat and confident. She didn't make threats to follow up her commands. She didn't need to. In a fight, Leah decided she'd definitely have to shoot Li Lau first.

"Patrick," Neal said without much effort. "If you will."

Silence.

Then a low vocal noise. Then steps. Four shoes scuffing a painted floor.

"So, Agent Capello," Oscar said. "If this painting is a fake, Neal here may have kidnapped Markov's child to keep its fakery a secret."

"Yes," Leah said.

"If it's real, he probably didn't."

"Probably not," Leah agreed.

"And you're going to have to put that glass down and apologize for being an ass."

"Or something." Leah's arm twitched. This position was starting to hurt.

Joshua entered the well-lit circle and stopped. He cupped his hands in front of him, the sheen of the leather driver's gloves exaggerated by the harsh lighting. When Leah met his eyes, he winked.

"Thank you, Patrick," Li Lau said.

"Yes," Piggy said. "I remember you now. I've seen you with Markov."

"Step up, Mr. Fawls," Oscar said. "Have a good, long look."

Neal stepped to the side. "Have at it."

Leah tossed the broken glass to the side. No one looked towards the tinkle. They all watched Joshua pull his right glove off, followed by his left. He reached around his torso and tucked them into the back pocket of his jeans. He approached the sketch, hands raised and fingers spread, as if he might tickle it.

He moved within an inch of the sketch. Ivory paper, reddish brown ink, thin lines, thick lines and hashing and shading. He pursed his lips and closed his eyes. Leah watched his fingertips. They all did. Everyone.

Almost everyone.

CHAPTER FORTY THREE

Leah knew art when she saw it. All kinds of art. A decent painting, a worthy sculpture, a piece of remarkable, thought-provoking performance art. Like this one: Joshua's approach to the supposed Michelangelo, with its tens of millions of dollars in weight. His charisma and showmanship, played under the lights, which had been perfectly arranged to force everyone's attention at a fine and fixed focal point.

Painters used focus to take a viewer down the path they wanted. Stage managers on Broadway understood the technique—look over here, not over there, and voilà—the stage is set. Magician's used the trick to its fullest—focus that misdirects. Leah only recently realized that improv troupes worked this way, too, sometimes, to keep the audience engaged, to keep the ball rolling, to turn a small ball of tension into laughs, then more laughs and ultimately a snowball of riot.

Neal used the trick to mask his escape. He faded into the black.

Leah ran.

She knew, in her head, the direction of the main entrance. Thank God, because the work lights had shrunken her pupils to the point of uselessness in the dark. She hoped Neal didn't know about some exit she'd never seen. He might have. He might also not have had the fore-sight or chance. She reached the door and paused, holding her breath. She heard footsteps pounding the wooden stairs and flew, leaping down stairs, taking on more than her knees allowed. Pain just above the caps. Ignored.

She pivoted at the ground level. Neal didn't run for Brozilla's front door. She would've caught a glimpse. He must have gone farther, into the basement levels. Why? No time to answer. She ran again. Down the next flight of stairs. Into the blackness.

Assessment: This was stupid. You didn't pursue at full speed, into a closed area, unarmed.

It was Neal, she said to herself. A putz.

She heard noise behind her. Someone, or ones, followed. She ran into the hallway of the basement level. She'd been here last night. Three rooms. Left, right and center. She'd met Scott and Van in the one to the right. A coke den or love nest or whatever.

The door at the far end was open. A dim light cut through the crack. She ran towards it as the door swung wide.

A man stepped out, leveling a gun. A presumed gun. It only caught a scrap of light as he raised it. He was backlit. Leah got a silhouette, light on detail. The height and stance told her this was not Neal.

"Don't move," he said. Clear. Maybe nervous.

She heard a bunch of crap behind her. Stomping feet.

"Oh," came Joshua's voice. "You mean both of us?"

"Nobody move," the man said.

Leah realized she should be dead. He should have shot her and she should be dead. She would've thought about it some more, but even more noise interfered. Behind Joshua. She glanced back, and Patrick stood behind them, gun raised. A crossfire. These guys weren't good, and still, sadly, quite effective.

Another silhouette appeared in the doorway at the end of the hall. Neal.

"You should've quit," he said.

"Tell me about it," Leah returned.

"Now I've got to kill you both."

"Not really," Leah said. "You don't gain much. The deal upstairs is dead. Everyone knows you took Markov's kid. Markov probably knows by now. Your best bet is to run. Run hard and fast."

"But you know the provenance," Neal said. "The history of my little art project here. You and the lovely Joshua put it all together. You will explain it to Markov and that will make it easier for him. See? I've got to burn my sketches."

"You want a dead FBI agent on your ticket, too?"

"Ha," Neal spat. "I'll take the FBI over Markov."

"What about both?" Leah reached behind her. She could feel the knob to the room on the right. "Both can't be better. Think about this, Neal." Leah raised her head. "Hey, Patrick? Other guy I haven't met yet, who I'm certain didn't sign up for killing a federal agent? This ain't worth a couple of grand."

"No," Neal said. "I'll have to settle up with them. They'll be well compensated."

"This won't make it to Unsolved Mysteries, boys. The Bureau doesn't give up. As you can see. I didn't give up. Otherwise I wouldn't be here, right? Am I right?"

"Patrick," Neal said. "You might want to back up the stairs for this."

Leah grabbed Joshua by the forearm with her left hand and cranked the knob with her right. She fell back into the love nest, pulling Joshua with her. They stumbled into the dark. She kicked the door closed.

"Get her!" She heard Neal shout.

Joshua turned on a light from a wall switch. Red, from the table between the two creepy couches. Leah spun. No other exit. No windows. Could she move the couches?

"She's unarmed, remember?" Neal shouted louder.

Joshua took the Ithaca shot gun from where it leaned against the wall and tossed it to her.

The shotgun from last night?

Joshua locked the door. Leah opened the breach. No shells.

The doorknob jiggled. Joshua walked backwards, keeping him-self between the door and Leah.

She dug the shells from the pocket of her jacket.

"Get them!" Neal shouted again.

"Move!" Leah shoved the shells into the gun. Top barrel and bottom.

The door smashed open. Two men, guns first. Leah clanked the gun closed, raised and pulled the trigger. The flash of the barrel flooded her view; the boom drowned out the world. Both men arched backwards out of the doorway.

She vaulted through the smoke and burnt acid smell. She saw spots. Her ears echoed bells. Patrick lay splattered across the hallway, spread like a gutted starfish. The other one leaned on his side. Some of the shot caught his gun arm. He moaned and squirmed.

Leah looked down the hall. Neal had ducked into the far room.

"Get the guns," Leah said. She failed to hear her voice. She moved forward, shotgun pressed firmly in the nook of her shoulder. She stopped at the entrance to the room, poked the barrels in and fanned the space.

Neal stood at the far wall, holding a four-year-old boy in front of him. Stepan junior cried silently. Trembling. Eyes red and streaming. Neal pressed a small, nickel-plated pistol to the boy's head.

"Neal," Leah said softly. "He's a little boy."

"You've left me no choice," Neal said. She thought he said. She got most of it from reading his lips. He looked like he wanted to cry along with the boy.

He's not getting away, she yammered in her head. *He's not getting away. He's not getting away.*

"It's going to be alright, Stepan," Leah said. "I'm going to take you home now."

"I think I'm leaving with the boy," Neal said.

He's not getting away.

"Or not," Leah lowered her shotgun thirty degrees. "All I want is the boy."

"That's all? I can walk out of here."

He's not getting away. He's not getting away.

Just like last time. All the other times.

No.

"Yes," Leah said. "Grab a drink on your way. I don't care."

"You're going to let me go?" Neal's face showed nothing but disbelief.

"That's what I said."

"Doesn't seem like you."

"Nope," Leah said. "This is all about you, Neal. I can stand here and wait until the police arrive. In this neighborhood, I'm thinking seven minutes. They hang at that coffee shop on 7th. Or you can take your head start."

Neal stared at her. Eyes blank. She thought it odd. Rather than deep in thought, he pretty much looked dead.

"Stepan," Leah said. "Why don't you come over here?"

Leah lowered the gun and held her left hand out to him.

Stepan didn't budge.

"Styopa," she half-sang. "I take you home now."

She positioned the shotgun behind her back and bent slightly at the waist. She smiled.

The boy looked at her. Eyeing her up. Scared, careful, confused. She didn't know. She didn't know shit about kids. She knelt down, tip of the gun barrel skidding across the floor behind her, and put her left arm straight out. "Styopa?"

Stepan Jr. walked towards her. Neal stood, gun pointed down at nothing. She took the child in her arms and pressed him against her. Neal blinked an extra long blink and dashed by her. She twisted and looked as Joshua stepped to the side, a pistol in each hand. They watched him hurdle two bodies and disappeared up the black, black stairs.

CHAPTER FORTY FOUR

Stepan Jr. sat on Leah's lap, gazing into the sparkle of the bottles lining the back of the bar. The bartender looked past her at the commotion she could hear and didn't need to see. Police, paramedics, none of her people yet. They were on their way, though. She knew that. They'd come with questions and she wasn't sure she had all the answers.

"Hey," she chirped at the bartender. "You know how to make a Shirley Temple?"

"Yeah." He shook himself out of his daze. "Yeah, sure." He made a show of it, so the kid could watch him twirl the glass and shaker, using far more effort than necessary, which she appreciated. Anything to keep Stepan Jr. distracted.

The New York Police Department questioned Joshua outside, out of her earshot. She would've done the same thing. Talk to her in a bit, see if their stories matched.

"I don't need Joshua, anyway," she told little Stepan. "I think I like you better."

The bartended slid over a heavy glass, paper umbrella sticking out of the red cocktail. He smiled.

"Thank you," Stepan Jr. said.

"You are very welcome, sir." He looked at Leah. "And for you?"

"I wish," Leah said.

"Yeah." He stepped back and returned his attentions to the mess.

Stepan Jr. picked up the glass with both hands and leaned in for a sip. He said, "Aaaa. It's good."

"I guess we'll stick around, then," Leah said. "And that's fine with me. I'm not in the mood to bar hop, if you know what I mean."

He took another sip.

Leah kept Stepan facing the bar as they rolled out at gurney carrying the gunman she'd got in the arm. He seemed stable. She redoubled her efforts to keep the little guy busy as they rolled out the other guy. He'd reached a stable state, too. Not the good kind.

Detective Roberts came up to the bar on Leah's left. The side not sporting a child. She'd met him the previous night, investigating the gallery heist Stepan Sr. faked. Last night? Was that really freakin' last night? It felt like two years ago. He put a Glock 17M .9mm on the bar in front of her.

"This yours?" he asked.

She looked at it. Flared at the bottom, like sailor's pants, no finger grooves, which she loved because she had small fingers and a lot of other guns were just plain uncomfortable—it was an FBI duty pistol. They all pretty much looked the same, but this weapon had a slight fade on the edge of the barrel that ended in three skip marks. Very faint, very district, very hers.

"Thanks." She took it and slipped it into the holster behind her hip. "Very kind of you."

"I know what it's like." He turned and leaned back against the bar. He wanted to monitor the activity as he talked. "Though it seems you did damn well without it."

"Not the way I like to do things," Leah replied.

"Looks like you took out two men with one shot and you weren't even armed."

"Well, when you say it that way."

"If you don't mind my asking, where'd you even get that long gun?"

"The boys should've frisked me better."

He chuckled. "This have anything to do with last night?"

"They're connected. Is that why you're here?"

"I heard your name. Your name's got a Major Crimes ring to it."

"I will be making a report," Leah said.

"We're cool."

"I'll make sure you're in the loop," she continued. "I know what it's like, too."

"Much appreciated," Roberts said.

Leah torqued her waist as far as it would allow, checking the activity behind her. They were almost done with the medical stuff. The NYPD wouldn't let Joshua back in to talk to her until they debriefed her. That wouldn't happen until Dean showed up. He came from the say-as-little-as-you-can branch of the Bureau. She came from the other. She hadn't met anyone else in her branch yet. In fact, she had the sense that the branch might close before the night ran out.

Dean entered the bar—white Polo shirt, mom jeans, badge stuck in his belt. He planted and pressed his hands to his hips, and panned the room, looking for his Spaniel that got into the neighbor's garden. He spotted her, frowned and started over. He opened his mouth. Leah's eye flared and a smile spread across her face.

Lidiya and Stepan Markov came through the doorway, hands clutched, faces just shy of panic.

"Hey, partner," Leah said as she spun on her bar stool, spinning Junior along with her. She slid him down the floor and sent him running at his running mom. Lidiya swept him up and crushed him to her. Leah thought the woman would press her baby right back into her. Stepan Sr. wrapped his arms around them both, eyes and mouth pulled tight. The handsome billionaire tough-guy essence left him like a ghost. He stood, hunched and hugging, withered and spent, peaceful and frayed.

Leah Capello was a special agent in the world's most powerful law enforcement agency. She would not cry, she would not cry, she would not cry—she would feel Dean's arm around her and bury her face in the crux of his shoulder.

And she would pull free a moment later. Crap, she needed mirror to see how crappity crap she looked. She cranked her head to catch a glimpse of herself in the mirror behind the bartender. She been rendered by Alberto Giacometti, black and silver, a wiry, figure stretched to the point of sag.

"We're, a, gonna need a statement," she heard from behind her. Bottles blocked the image of the male speaker.

"We're going to debrief her first," Dean returned.

"Yeah, it's just—"

"Yep," Dean said.

"It sounds like we still got someone outstanding."

"Neal Pozner," Leah said as she turned. She checked out the detective: Hispanic, male, six-two, two-hundred-ten pounds, khaki pants, white shirt, striped tie—a costume for him, no matter how well he wore it. Roberts talked to Stepan Sr. Again, just what she would've done. She rammed her backbone straight and drew back her shoulders. "Wanted for kidnapping. We're on it."

"Can you give us a moment?" Dean said to the detective.

The detective gave them the slow blink and backed off, out of earshot to them, into earshot of the Roberts and the Markovs.

Dean put his head close, cocked to the right, so the gentlemen of the NYPD had no chance of reading his lips. "The kidnapper got away?"

"He won't get far," she said.

"We need to mobilize."

"Totally," Leah said. "God forbid Markov gets to him first."

"Are you going to be alright?" Dean asked, with a quizzical squirm of his eyebrows.

"Never better."

"You killed a man," Dean said. "That never goes down easy."

"Saved a little boy," Leah said. "That's a freakin' spoon full of sugar."

They sat saying nothing for a handful of seconds. They watched the Markovs get ushered outside. A couple of crime scene guys strolled in with their kits, ready to swipe and brush and photograph. A uniformed officer took up a position by the door. They were going to be here for a while.

"Maybe we could talk in the morning," Leah said.

"Yep," Dean replied.

They walked outside, into the storm of blinking red and blue. The cops had plugged the street with yellow tape. Cars and people tried to get a better look at the clog or tried to get around it, pissed off that New York had, once again, kept them from their personal point B. Leah peered up and down the street in both directions. She didn't see Joshua anywhere.

"You need a lift?" Dean asked.

She'd forgotten about him. "No. I've still got a car."

"You're sure you're alright?"

"No, I've still got car."

"See?" Dean said. "That's what I mean."

Leah stopped searching up and down the street, and gave Dean a fake smile. He wouldn't catch it in this deluge of color. "I'm worse than I think, but better than you think. Give me a night and we'll see how I've held up. K?"

Dean gave her a fake smile. Despite the flashing lights, she totally caught it.

CHAPTER FORTY FIVE

Leah put the FBI sedan in a slot that was very close to being legal. The trunk intruded into a driveway, but she firmly believed a car could still get around it. At least any car that might try in the next ten hours. She walked towards the front of her building. The temperature had dropped to a slight chill, her biochemistry dropped to a damn cold slog. She could feel her blood going to sleep even as she pushed it through her leg muscles.

A figure sat on one of the two steps leading to her front door. Nonchalant. Leaning out, relaxed, arms on his knees, too cocky for a mugger, just cocky enough for a dealer, though she'd never seen one working this block. He better not be some lowlife. She had nothing left in her for lowlifes. She'd have to shoot him and mop up in the morning.

"I'm very glad they didn't keep you much longer," Joshua said.

Leah let her body droop. "Not as glad as me."

"Almost nodded off."

"You should've gone home."

"Wasn't ready for that," Joshua said. "You know how it is with house guests."

"Marisa, right." Leah stopped in front of him. "Although she's not like a cousin in from the country."

"She's stayed too long just the same."

"Oh, so that's how it is."

"No. I mean, you don't know how it is."

Leah crossed her arms. "I'm not inviting you up."

"I just wanted to make sure you were all right."

"Now you know. Fit as a rain."

Joshua smiled up at her, the corners of his mouth like two little shepherd crooks, perfect for hooking lost lambs. Sheep, counting sheep.

"You're an art thief," Leah said.

"Who said that? Neal?"

"He said the Bacon painting was stolen."

"Maybe, maybe not." Joshua leaned back on the pavement so he didn't have to knock his head back to speak with her. "Things come into my possession. Whether I want them to or not, sometimes. It's a side-effect."

"A side-effect of the drugs you're on? Or I'm on, and don't even know it?"

Joshua patted the concrete next to him. "Can you believe that shotgun was still there?"

"That was unbelievably lucky." Leah sat down on the concrete next to him.

"That's how it works sometimes." Joshua looked at the cars lumbering by. "In the big flow of things."

"That's never how it works." Leah stared out into the hum of the city.

"Marisa, the shotgun—sometimes things I touch stay in my orbit."

Leah turned towards him. Their faces only inches apart and she still couldn't tell the bull from the shit. With a face like his, it could be so easy to push the words aside. Talking was one thing lips could do, and not the most interesting.

"You kissed that shotgun," Leah said as she remembered.

"Yes," Joshua replied.

"For luck?"

"It's probably how the tradition started. Someone like me, deep in the past, kissed his desires into something—a precious sword and the sword came back to him. A charm."

"A charm," Leah said. "As in charming."

"Everything's linked," Joshua returned.

"You kissed Marisa."

"In a moment of weakness, some time ago."

"You kissed my badge. The first time we met."

"It just works better that way."

"What does, Joshua? What works better?"

"I can read objects," Joshua said. "I can write a little, too. I can make sure they are part of my future. If I really want something, I can make an impression. I wanted to see you again, so I juiced your badge. I took a chance with the shotgun. The way things were going, I thought it might come in handy. Of course, I didn't know exactly how the gun would come back to me. It could've been the troublesome end."

"And Marisa?" Leah whispered.

"People are stuff." Joshua reached a hand to her face. He touched her left cheek with the soft leather of his glove. "Very com-plicated stuff."

Leah felt heat beneath the cool leather. She opened her mouth, let some air in and said, "Does that line ever work?"

Joshua returned his hands to his knees. "I wouldn't know. Making an impression on a Francis Bacon painting is one thing. Impressing a person leads to Marisa."

"If you want . . ." Leah let the thought knock around in her weary head. A dryer on slow. With one sneaker inside. He said he wanted to see her again and then another part, about touching. "You believe all this?"

"I've been living all of this."

"You know paintings resurface frequently in our world," Leah said. "And not too many people use that basement room at Brozilla on a Thursday. And Marisa could be an obsessive, possessive narcissist all on her own. I went to high school with a bunch you never kissed."

"As far as you know," Joshua added.

"As far as I know," Leah agreed.

"What about your badge?"

"If you were an art thief and a conman," Leah said, "we'd eventually run into each other."

"Well, it couldn't have happened at a better time." Joshua rose and stuck out his hand. Leah took it, used it and they strolled towards the front doors of her apartment building.

"Still not inviting you up."

"As far as you know," Joshua added.

"As far as I know," Leah agreed.

ABOUT THE AUTHOR

Michael J. Martineck has written for DC Comics, *The Truth About Cars*, short stories, and long stories. Michael's novel—*The Milkman* (EDGE Science Fiction and Fantasy), a murder mystery set in a world with no governments—won a gold medal from the Independent Publisher Book Awards and was a finalist in the Eric Hoffer awards. His previous novel, *Cinco de Mayo*, was a finalist for an Alberta Reader's Choice Award. He has also written two urban fantasy novels for young readers. Michael has a master's degree in English, an undergraduate degree in Economics, but has worked in advertising for years and years. He lives with his wife and two children on Grand Island, NY.

Other books by Michael J. Martineck

Cinco de Mayo
Alberta Readers Choice Award Finalist
"His writing flows naturally, his characters speak as if they were real people, and his setting seems so real that I wouldn't be surprised to find it on a normal, everyday roadmap. I wound up being firmly convinced that this place, these people, are real and living just out of sight, somewhere . . ." - Dan L. Hollifield

The Milkman
Gold Medal – IPPY for Best Science Fiction Novel
Eric Hoffman Awards Finalist, Best Novel
" . . . an impressive demonstration of the author's skills." *Publishers Weekly*

The Link Boy
"If you enjoyed '1984' by Orwell, 'The Space Merchants' by Kornbluth and Pohl, or "The Windup Girl' by Bacigalupi', you will love this book." - Ralph Kerminski